First T_

'A gripping portrayal of a fourteen-year-old girl stumbling, unprepared, into an adult world . . . extremely well written . . . it has a deeply genuine feel to it'

Carolyn Hart, *Financial Times*

'Harte has got it absolutely right. It's raw, slightly grubby, and spectacularly well observed' Christie Hickman, *Midweek*

'Harte conveys the desperate earnestness of it all . . . There is a concentrated skill and a conviction in the voice'

Maggie Traugott, *Independent on Sunday*

Losing It

'Harte . . . has lost none of her skill at describing the sullen fear of outwardly streetwise youth. [She] writes with stunning conviction; you are not very far into the book before you feel that you know the inside of the Murphys' home, with its cheap ornaments and constantly flowing vodka, as well as your own' Penny Perrick, *The Times*

'An assured and confident work: Lara Harte has the gift of being able to describe emotional states with economy. The novel is unpretentious, authentic and enthralling'

Times Literary Supplement

Lara Harte was born in Dublin in 1975, where she still lives. She graduated in English and French from University College, Dublin, in 1997. She wrote *First Time* when she was eighteen. Her second novel, *Losing It*, is also available in Phoenix paperback.

First Time

LARA HARTE

PHŒNIX

A PHOENIX PAPERBACK

First published in Great Britain by Phoenix House in 1996
This paperback edition published in 1997 by Phoenix,
an imprint of Orion Books Ltd,
Orion House, 5 Upper St Martin's Lane,
London WC2H 9EA

Reissued 2000

Copyright © Lara Harte 1996

A CIP catalogue record for this book
is available from the British Library.

ISBN 1 85799 836 7

Printed and bound in Great Britain by
The Guernsey Press Co. Ltd, Guernsey, C.I.

For my family

CHAPTER I

Beautiful day, soft, sultry, sunny, September. God knows, for going back to school you'd think at least the weather'd take pity on me. Explode into a hurricane so I'd know that something anyway, felt like I did. Take a leaf from the book of winter, so that the bright, cheery worshippers of the sun, throwing back the curtains to greet a clear blue sky, would reach forward and feel instead the bitter cold leaping up to bite them, seeping through their blood and chilling them. Reminding them that this is the winter and they can't have everything their own way.

The first day back at an exclusive all-girls' private secondary school in a 'sought-after' location, not too far from the city-centre, twenty minutes of a brisk walk, make that five to ten minutes by bus in light traffic, hurtling by the rambling Victorian houses – detached, semi-detached, and terraced. Some of the houses are subdivided into flats, rented out to students and single people. Others are owned by fortunate families. In the streets closest to the city-centre they are used as offices. The cost of these houses has shot up in the last few years, so the families who live here are well off, and they have very privileged children, like me. Like the others from around here who go to my renowned school.

I am a privileged child. The only child of parents who have stayed together. A successful businessman father. Nice, convenient set-up, ideal, really. The perfect stage for the perfect rôle. What happens when you've got the wrong girl for the part?

We moved here two years ago when I was twelve. It was the summer before I started at this secondary school, and my parents congratulated themselves on their timing. That September, everyone else of my age would share the excitement, trauma and insecurity of a new school. It would be easy for me to make lots of nice new friends. Their unspoken worry that I wouldn't panicked and undermined me, made me feel even less confident, so I refused to discuss the subject. I banished the thought of school, and remembered the friends from our old street: Cliona and Elizabeth and Christina. We had lived in a little grey house in a large estate of identical houses in a sprawling suburb called Carrickglass, ten miles from the city centre. That was before we were well off. I walked in through the gates of the new school in the same grey skirt and navy jumper that I am wearing today, exactly two years later, thinking almost the same thoughts now as I did then. Now that Aisling is gone, I'm almost back where I started. Aisling was my only friend, from the first day, until two months ago, when she went to live in America.

I've heard people, parents, teachers, and classmates remark, both to us, and to each other, what a strange, withdrawn and quiet pair we made, how shy we must be, seeing as we didn't really mix with the rest of the class. This annoyed us. We weren't shy. We just didn't like anyone else,

2

and we wanted to be left alone. We didn't have anything against them, just found it hard to talk to them.

Our Class, the A-stream, was boring; all they ever did was work. We divided them into open swots and closet swots. The open swots did not conceal the fact that they spent every waking moment studying. I didn't mind them so much. They were at least honest about it. It was the ones who claimed that they hadn't even looked at a book before a test and then came out with high marks that annoyed me. They'd say their essays were too short and looked a mess – and then produce page upon page upon page of beautifully written arguments, and so on. Even Linda and Natasha, the so-called rebels who 'skimped' on their work, stayed safely within the acceptable limits of the A-stream in a school with high academic standards. People travelled from far-off suburbs just to attend our school. It was very difficult to get into.

As I approached the school gates, blue, cheerful, flung open in welcome, I saw Sinéad and Tessa and went over to them. They were always nice; of the open swot variety. I was taller than them now, by about a head. Sinéad looked up at me in surprise, and I saw myself and my grey eyes reflected in her glasses.

'God, Cassandra, you've grown so tall.'

'I know.'

'And your hair's gone so long,' Tessa said, discarding a strand of her own hair upon examination. 'I've been trying to grow mine all summer, and it just won't grow. It's not fair. Sinéad's has, and she doesn't even want hers to grow.'

Tessa's reddish-brown hair was still as shoulder-lengthish as ever, a fringe framing her broad, freckled face. Sinéad's was looking better than usual, the sun having brought goldy highlights out in it. I knew it must have been the sun; she'd never even put a light rinse in her hair, but I asked, just to make sure. Yes, the sun. Did I really think it was nice? Mine was nice too, she said. Thick and fair, like a model's. Some people would break their hearts and their banks trying to get it like that. They were particularly friendly today, guessing that I was missing Aisling, and I was grateful to them for that.

At assembly we learnt that Miss Healy, our English teacher, would also be our class tutor. They seemed happy enough with that. She was thirtyish, approachable and fond of homework. We had her last year and everybody liked her. I didn't particularly care one way or the other. School was school and teachers were all much of a muchness really.

Sinéad and Tessa sat at a table in the middle of the room, and I was invited to sit at the empty desk behind them. It was a safe enough position, not beside the window so the sun couldn't hurt my eyes, not too near the door for the draughts in winter, and not too near the front to be constantly called upon by the teachers.

No sooner had we sat down than shrieks erupted behind us to the right. I looked behind and my eye was almost knocked out by Linda's elbow as she ran to the front of the room chased by Natasha who caught her and struggled with her for the possession of a plastic, red, see-through cigarette lighter, her bun bopping up and down, the little black bun at the back of her head that all her thin, scraggy hair was scraped and glued into.

'Bitch!' she shrieked. 'Give it back, you fucking cow!'

A little later she emerged, successfully clasping the holy grail, hair completely unruffled, although she ran her hands

4

over it anxiously. They looked round as if surprised to see everyone staring at them, though I knew very well that their little show had been staged exclusively for our benefit.

'She took my Gary's lighter,' Natasha said significantly, as if that explained everything, and as if we were all supposed to know exactly what she was talking about.

'Your Gary? Don't you mean your ex-Gary?' Linda asked, red-faced, red-freckled, sympathetically patting her on the shoulder and rolling her eyes at the audience.

She shook her immaculately maintained red corkscrew curls back from her face. 'It was only a joke, you didn't have to freak out or anything.'

They went back to their desk, muttering to each other.

Tessa eyed them scornfully. 'I see the rebels are back,' she said sarcastically. 'They just put it all on to show off. I wish they'd cop on to themselves.'

'They'll have to if they want to pass the Junior Cert,' Sinéad replied.

Tessa looked horrified at the mention of exams. 'Our first day back and you're already talking about exams! Isn't it bad enough having to study for them without having to talk about them as well.' They grimaced in mutual resignation at the gruesome year which lay ahead.

I felt a wave of resentment. It was the typical hypocritical attitude of my class. They all pretended that they were forced to do well in school to get the points to get into college. It wasn't that they wanted to do it, they just had to. They annoyed me, not so much because of what they did, but because of the way they went on about it. Nobody was forcing them to work themselves into the ground. They did it of their own free will. So I resented their attitude, open

5

swots and closet swots alike, mainly because they made me feel guilty. Guilty because I shared their anxiety about exams and the future, but not their zeal for studying. Guilty when they showed me up. Angry at them for making me feel guilty.

Not that I wasn't bright. On the contrary, things came relatively easily to me, and I knew that by normal standards I worked hard. But *they* weren't normal. I couldn't rise to their level no matter what, but it still annoyed me when everyone else studied harder and got higher marks. I knew that if I worked any harder I'd have no time to myself, or, in the past, to spend with Aisling. But Aisling was gone now, and with the Junior Cert this year, our class would be worse than ever. The atmosphere would be unbearable.

Healy came into the room with a girl I didn't recognise; a new girl. Not pretty, but quite striking because of her jet-black hair which reached down to her waist. It was very thin and a bit dry looking, but that didn't matter because of its colour. She had it tied up at the front, and was wearing make-up. That made a change; only Linda and Natasha ever wore make-up to school. She had blue eyeliner and grey eyeshadow on pale blue eyes that were round and small. She had a long face and a long nose. She was introduced to us as Emma O'Toole, and told to sit next to me. As we would keep the same places in every class, this meant I would be sitting with her for the rest of the year.

'Hi, I'm Cassandra,' I said, as she installed herself beside me.

'Your hair's gorgeous,' she exclaimed, and I returned the compliment, pulling at my own in surprised delight, trying

6

to conceal this in half-embarrassment that she'd notice and think I was vain or weird or both. My thick blonde hair, not as long as hers, but long, and much thicker.

Healy busied herself drawing the seating plan, so we were free to talk. Tessa and Sinéad turned around and introduced themselves. Emma lived in Kilmore, and had gone to school there – only her parents had always wanted her to go here. She finally got in when someone left.

'That was my friend Aisling. She went to live in America.'

'You must miss her, so. I know I feel bad enough not being able to see my friends at school anymore. I don't know what I'd do if they actually left the country.'

'What was your other school like?'

She smiled in recollection. 'It's a deadly place, it's mixed, and everyone in it's a header. You don't know how sorry they were for me when I told them I was coming to this kip. They said it'd be full of dry-arsed snobs. Is it?'

There was an embarrassed silence. Sinéad and Tessa looked insulted.

'Sorry. I didn't mean to say the wrong thing.'

'That's all right, and we're not actually that bad. We even have our rebels, Linda and Natasha,' Sinéad said, pointing them out.

'Then there's Nuala and Nora in front of them, who hang around with them, only they're quieter versions,' Tessa added.

Then there was another short silence. The teacher started talking about the coming year. Emma wrote me a note. 'I don't think Sinéad and Tessa like me very much.'

'Don't worry about them,' I whispered.

'I'm not. They're dry-arses anyway,' she whispered back. 'What are Linda and Natasha like?'

Healy looked over at us. 'That's enough chat down there!'

Emma made a face at me, and I wrote on the side of my copy 'poseurs and ravers'. She rolled her eyes upwards.

A few minutes later, Healy put the time-table up on the board for us to take down. Emma seized the opportunity to say, 'I'm nothing in particular. I'm a bit of a hippy, and I love grunge, and I'm sort of a gothic, as I wear a lot of black, only there's not a lot of them left in Kilmore. There's loads and loads of ravers, which some of my friends are, but I can't stand the music. I have some rocker friends, but there's not a lot of them left either, and I hate their music too except for Metallica – "Enter Sandman" 's my favourite song, and I love Guns' n' Roses as well, but my all-time favourites are The Doors. What about you?'

I was a bit taken aback by all this. 'Like yourself I suppose. Everything and nothing.'

Me and Aisling didn't think much of the music that was around, but we had liked the hippy clothes, as well as the black gothic clothes, and had worn some of them – innocuous and popular things like loads of black, as well as tie-dyed and multi-coloured, long and loose. Nothing extreme, ever, though we had often eyed groups of such girls enviously when we were in town, ravers and all (they were mainly ravers now, only we didn't like their clothes), and longed to be amongst them. What exciting lives they must have, we'd think, the wild nights they must spend knacker-drinking in fields, big gangs of them (that was supposed to be the best crack going), and the gorgeous boyfriends they must be able to pick and choose from. My old friend Christina,

8

now Queen of the Carrickglass Ravers, had told us all about it when we ran into her in town last Christmas, the first time I'd seen her since I'd moved away.

'None of youse drink where youse live?' she'd asked in disbelief, as she clutched her Joe Bloggs top tightly around her to keep out the bitter, damp, winter wind.

'Well some people say they do, only they sort of like get drunk on half a can,' I'd said scornfully, attempting to gain some of her respect.

'You poor thing. That's what you get for moving to some mad snobby place.' I haven't seen her since.

Kilmore, from what I've heard, is a lot like Carrickglass, only much nearer here. In fact, their buses even pass through here on their way to town. Emma must live such a life, I thought, looking at her with a mixture of envy and awe. I took note of the little red hole at the base of her left nostril, which was facing me, and counted six similar holes in her left ear, and I tried to imagine how amazing she would look outside school.

The class ended, and everyone crowded around our desk, wanting to introduce themselves to Emma. By the time we'd made our way to the next class, most people had said a few words. When we sat at our new desks, Linda and Natasha came to pay their dues, assessing Emma with their eyes, hers assessing them in return.

'What do you think of this place?' Natasha asked, sitting on Sinéad and Tessa's vacant desk with Linda squeezing in beside her.

'It's alright,' Emma was now being cautious.

'Yeah, it's alright,' Linda said disparagingly. 'Bit of a kip though.'

Emma acknowledged this with her face but said nothing. She was probably sick of talking about school. She'd already asked and learnt about all the teachers, which ones were good, bad, nice, terrible, which subjects were a doss. She wasn't pleased to hear that nothing was a doss, that we got loads of homework, and were expected to do lots of study on top of that, that there were tests in everything all the time. Nuala, who had been described to her as a 'lesser rebel', explained earnestly to Emma that frequent testing was really a good thing, because it forced you to learn thoroughly even the subjects you hated, and constantly going over something made you really understand it. Emma shot me a look of horror and I returned one of empathy.

'Are these people for real?' she muttered to me as we sat down.

Yes, the place was a kip, although the building itself and the grounds were actually very nice. The structure was bright, airy, modern, with big windows and big white classrooms. In winter, the rooms were always warm, except close to the doors, which were constantly opening and closing. We had a large dining hall, and an indoor gym. Outside there were hockey pitches, tennis and basketball courts, and a running track. It was a pity I didn't like sport; neither did Emma. I only liked swimming, and as a child I'd loved my ballet lessons. Emma whispered to me that she was exactly the same, only she kept the ballet a secret, because she would get such a slagging in Kilmore if it ever came out. Those she'd been friends with since she was a kid had forgotten, and she liked it that way.

I was thrilled to receive such a confidence. I liked her, and I felt she might like me too.

CHAPTER 2

Emma and I stuck close together for the rest of the morning. By the time school finished at half-twelve, I had told her all about Aisling, and she in turn had told me all about her wonderful friends at her old school, and in particular, her best friend, Brenda.

Emma hadn't wanted to come to this school at all. She had threatened to run away, move in with Brenda, leave school and get a job. I was impressed. I would never dare talk to my parents like that. Not that they were strict or anything (in fact, they were reasonable about everything), but I knew very well that talk like that would get me killed. Emma, however, threatened and pleaded and tantrummed to no avail. Her mother wanted her to get a good education in a good school full of nice girls, not like that crowd of knackers she hung around with. How dare she say that about her friends, Emma had shouted; not to mention saying it about Brenda, her best friend since she was a kid, her mam's own friend's daughter. Or maybe she'd got it wrong, maybe Mam was only using her because there was no one better around. 'That's not what I meant and you know it,' Mam said back, real insulted. 'I meant the rest of that crowd of yours. Brenda is welcome in this house anytime, as is her mother. I'm appalled you could even think such a thing.'

I was astonished. 'You mean she didn't hit the roof?'

Emma looked smug. 'No she didn't. My mam's like that, she never freaks out or anything. And my da does whatever she says. He always leaves that sort of stuff for her to sort out. I never see him anyway. He's always at work, and when he does come home he's in a pisser of a mood, so I stay well away from him.'

'That's awful.' I was horrified.

'What is? That I stay away from him?' she asked defensively.

'No, that you don't seem to get on with either of your parents.'

'Oh, it's not that I don't get on with them, I do. Well, I get on well enough with my mam when she's not annoying me, and she's the one who's always at home, and I do what I want most of the time anyway, so . . .' she shrugged.

'So, how come you ended up here then?' I was more than a little jealous.

'There wasn't much I could do about it. My old school had been told I wasn't coming back, my old uniform sold and my new one bought on the sly by my mam, this term's fees paid for here, and the books got. So, I figured there was no way out of it. The best thing I could do was give in, reluctantly, and in great pain, and get what I could out of them in return.'

Amazement was probably written all over my face.

'Well, what do you expect?' she asked with an air of

12

bitterness. 'If they treat me like shit, I'll treat them like shit.'

I felt ashamed of myself. She had obviously been very upset by her parents' treatment of her. I would have been, too, in her shoes. She was probably putting on a lot of that cold cynicism to cover up how bad she was really feeling. In fact, something in her face seemed to be telling me that she wanted me to know this, even though it was too distressing for her to word it herself. I gave her an understanding look, and felt privileged to be trusted with her real feelings.

After school, she couldn't wait to get out of the place. I was to walk her to the bus stop as it was on my way home. As soon as we were out of the class she took her hair down – she hated having to tie it up and couldn't believe they were making her do it.

As soon as we were outside the gates, she grabbed my arm. 'God, I need a cigarette after that,' she said, as if this was the longed-for reward for coming through a great ordeal.

I had suspected that she might smoke, those wild types often did.

'You'd never know you smoked; you can't smell it off you at all,' I exclaimed admiringly.

'That's because I'm very careful.' She was pleased at the compliment. 'I'd be dead if the oul pair ever found out, so I have mints to take the smell off my breath – only you have to take loads of them, real strong ones, or they don't work.'

She brandished a can of deodorant taken from her bag.

'This is for my clothes, and I used bleach to get the yellow stuff off my fingers. It works great. One rub and they're snow white again.'

'Where's safe?' she continued, surveying the street with a practiced eye as we walked along.

I considered this. 'Those who smoke tend to go up a lane around the corner, only that's dangerous, because everyone can see them if they look up there, and last year, the teachers started going up there and catching them.'

'I don't want to get snared,' she sounded terrified. 'Is there nowhere else we can go?'

'I have the perfect place,' I assured her. 'And no-one else ever goes there.'

I led her to the spot me and Aisling had always thought would be the best place to smoke (if, of course, we smoked). To get to it, you go to the street around the corner from the school and up a lane which runs between two rows of three-storey red-brick houses. This leads to another lane, divided from the gardens backing on to it by two high concrete walls. There are no back entrances to the houses, which makes them more deserted. When you follow the lane to the left for about two minutes, you come to a short sharp bend which leads out, via another lane, onto the road. This little stretch was the perfect spot for the wary smoker, because, if someone was spied walking up the lane, the cigarette could be put out or hidden without being seen. But no-one ever smoked here, probably because it was open-ended. The girls from school liked dead-ends, where nobody would be walking up and down. Problem was, everyone knew what they were doing there.

All this I explained to Emma as we made our way there. She already had a cigarette in her mouth and a lighter held up to it as she sank down on her schoolbag with her back to the wall. She hungrily inhaled about half of it within about two seconds, and then she blew it out again in one long, calm and relaxed movement, stretching her feet out on the dusty concrete ground.

'God, I needed that,' she said, and took a smaller, less frantic drag. 'Do you want a smoke?' she asked, offering me the packet.

I had anticipated something like this, and answered as planned, with a casual, unapologetic, yet unaccusatory, 'No, I don't smoke.'

She appeared neither surprised nor displeased, and she put the packet back down beside her. 'You're dead right. They'll probably be the death of me, only there's no way I'd ever give them up. I love them too much.'

She blew smoke rings in my direction. 'Keep sketch then, will you, in case there's someone coming.'

I was relieved that she'd passed no heed of me. 'How long have you been smoking?' I asked, watching her light up another one.

'I'd say about a year now. Properly that is. Before that it was just now and then.'

'And how much do you smoke a day?'

'It depends on the money, and what Brenda can nick off her ma and da, and what we can scab off other people . . .'

'Brenda robs cigarettes off her parents!'

Emma burst out laughing. 'It's not like that. Both her parents smoke like troopers, and they're always leaving loads of open boxes of twenties lying around, and they can never remember how many smokes they have, so of course we're going to take some. What do you expect us to do, just leave them there?' She looked at me with reproof for thinking her a common thief.

I hastened to move on. 'So, about how many then, would you usually smoke?'

'Well, on a school day, I'd have one in the mornings before going in. And then I can't have one again until after school, because it's obviously not safe to have one during lunch in this school . . .'

'Especially not in the toilets, they're always looking in there,' I warned her.

'It's the same everywhere. So, anyway, I'd probably have one after school, and then a couple more when I'm out with Brenda in the evening. I smoke much more at the weekends though, and whenever I go out, like drinking or something, I always have two packs of ten, and they're gone by the end of the night, and that's with keeping one packet hidden so that they're not all scabbed.'

'You mean you have to hide them so that you don't have to give them to other people?'

'More or less, yeah, well people are always wanting other people to give them smokes, so you just have to hide them and pretend you don't have any.'

It sounded like a vicious way of operating, but then most people our age wouldn't have that much money to spend on cigarettes, and they were a lot poorer out in Kilmore, and they had to buy their drink as well.

Emma tossed her butt away and picked up her bag. 'We'd better head. You're still walking me to the bus stop, aren't you?'

'Yes.'

'Good,' she said, with cheerful emphasis.

We began to make our way out of the lane.

'Do many people from school smoke?'

'Not many. Linda and Natasha are the only ones in our class, then there's maybe three or four from the other classes altogether. I think they're all friends with each other, they all smoke together anyway. I've seen them all going up the smoking lane. Then there's some girls from the higher years. That's about it really.'

'I thought as much. They're all such sad bitches. I am going to be bored out of my pisser in this school. No-one ever does anything. They all just sit there looking dopey and licking the arses off the teachers.'

'I know exactly what you mean. They say that school's boring for them, too, but somehow, I just don't think so.'

'How do you stand it?'

'You don't.'

Emma looked as if I'd just confirmed what she had long suspected to be the miserable truth.

'It wasn't as bad when Aisling was here, but she's gone now.'

'Well, we'll just have to stick together then.'

I was elated. We walked into the main street.

'Nice shops,' Emma said. 'I'd say they're expensive enough, though.'

We had now reached the bus stop, and Emma examined her time-table. We sat on the low adjacent wall to wait for the bus.

Emma's thoughts soon resumed their previous pattern. 'I bet you they're just as bad outside school,' she said. 'I bet you they wear really crappy clothes and have never had a drink or got off with a fella in their lives.'

I was at a loss for words. I agreed with her sentiments, but I didn't want to admit that, in those terms, I was probably almost as bad as they were, although I had the mitigating excuse of having spent a lot of time wishing to God that I wasn't; that I was somebody like Emma; and my clothes weren't as bad as theirs. Fortunately, I didn't have to respond as her bus came into view then, it was a good bit down the road, and had just stopped at the traffic lights.

Emma stood up. 'Now, I am going to go home to my mam who will want to know how exciting the new school is. Then I'll have to do my homework – imagine getting some on the first day, we never did in my last school – and my parents are going to be real strict about studying this year, what with the Junior Cert and the state of my summer report, and all the fees they're paying out. Then I might actually get to go out with Brenda. God, I can't wait till next summer.'

By now the bus had arrived. She got on it and I waved her off.

I was delighted with the possibilities which now opened up. Things would be better with Emma around. She really did like me, she had said so herself. I wanted to be really good friends with her. I wanted to be friends with all her other friends, and be able to go out with them. I wanted them to like me and treat me as one of them. But I feared them seeing me as they saw everyone else from school. I was afraid that even Emma would hold it against me that I had never gone drinking or had a boyfriend. I hoped against hope she wouldn't, as I made my way home.

I live in a three-storey house with my parents. It's beautiful. The ground floor is of grey granite, and has a separate front door, which is the one we use, under the flight of steps which leads up to the other front door. The other two storeys are red brick. On the bottom floor, there is a big living room to the front of the house, a toilet, and a large kitchen with french windows opening onto the conservatory which opens onto the back garden. The kitchen is roomy and bright, and we eat all our meals there. Upstairs, there is a long corridor which runs along the edge of the house from the stairs to the other front door. To the right is my dad's study, which overlooks the back garden, and the sitting room, which faces the street and is only used for visitors and at Christmas and stuff.

The bedrooms are on the top floor – mine at the back, my parents' and the small spare one to the front. And of course, there's the bathroom. There are fireplaces in all the rooms, wrought-iron ones in the bedrooms, and marble in the others. Mine is painted white and blue and there is a large mirror above it in a plain gold frame. In the alcove on one side of the fireplace is a wardrobe, and in the other there's a desk with shelves above it. On the other wall is my dressing table, a book case for my normal books, and a press with my stereo on it. My bed is set against the inside wall near the door. I have a blue carpet and white walls, and no pictures on the walls. I like my room, it was done up the way I wanted it.

Both my parents were in when I got home, as I had expected. My mum hasn't worked since before I was born, and my dad, the businessman, sometimes works from home with his computery thing and fax machine. They were in the kitchen having lunch.

'What kept you?' Mum asked, looking at the clock. It was pretty late.

'I was waiting at the bus stop with the new girl, Emma.'

'Oh I see. Is she nice?' she asked.

They had been encouraging me all summer to invite over some of the girls from school. The last thing they would have expected was for me to befriend a new girl.

'Aren't they nice girls?' they had said.

'They're alright, but they're boring.'

'I'm sure they can't all be boring. You should give people a chance.'

'Maybe I should change schools.'

'It would be the same anywhere else, because the problem is you, not them. You should make more of an effort.'

And then they'd look at me anxiously. Oh well, they should be happy now. I sat down and told them about Emma (the censored version), and they told me that that was great.

CHAPTER 3

The first week passed. Emma was quiet enough in class, did her homework and paid attention, apart from the occasional note written to me expressing boredom. On one of our daily after school visits up the lane, she confided in me that she was behaving herself to get her parents off her back. They were threatening her with dire punishments should she slip up. She had been constantly in and out of trouble at her last school and had failed practically all her summer tests. They were desperate that she should get on in life, and never let her forget that her dad was slaving away to pay fees that they could scarcely afford. There was nothing wrong with her last school, but her classmates were a bad influence on her, and the average intelligence was quite low, so Emma could not exercise her abilities to the full. This, Emma told me scornfully, was the sort of shit her mother, in particular, went on with. I felt very sorry for her, my own family situation being completely different, although we were both only children. I got on well with my parents and was allowed to do pretty much what I wanted, although there was of course nothing to do, living as I did in a dead area.

By this stage I had realised that Emma was actually only averagely bright, which in my definition means someone who, after slogging their guts out at their books for months, achieves no more than a respectable result. Nothing to be knocked by any means, but I also knew instinctively that Emma would not put in that kind of effort. She was too much her own person for that. She did not want to work excessively so she didn't. She (usually) did what she wanted. She sensed my admiration and was pleased. There was an easiness and a sort of natural complicity between us. We were fast becoming close friends, as I had longed for.

She was very wary about the rest of the class when they volunteered friendliness towards her. She was nice and polite to them with a touch of condescension, discernible to me because I knew what she felt, and picked up on by them, consciously or unconsciously though they didn't say anything. A combination of that, her 'mad' attitude and disgust at the school itself and school in general turned them away after initial attempts at friendship. They seemed to feel quite awkward around her. None of them knew what to say to her and she certainly had nothing to say to them.

At first Linda and Natasha made some offhand and condescending advances towards her. On Emma's second day, they approached us in the dining hall at lunchtime and sat down opposite us. They divided their time between telling Emma how boring school was and how gorgeous Gary, Natasha's ex-boyfriend, was, during and between mouthfuls of food. Natasha was going to get him back. He hadn't been around Cue lately, but the one time he had been there they had actually been talking to each other, and it had gone very well too. Cue was the amusement arcade in Crossgrange, where they lived, about three miles from the school.

What was his second name, Emma wondered, and who did he hang around with. Her friend Michelle's cousin, Gráinne Murphy, lived in Crossgrange and once when she was in town she had met Gráinne and her boyfriend and some of his friends.

Linda and Natasha had never heard of Gráinne; Emma had never heard of Gary either. Emma said that Gráinne had said that the people who lived in Crossgrange were mainly saps, but that, unlike here in Ashford, there were actually some decent people there too. That was very true, Linda and Natasha agreed wholeheartedly. But she had also said, strangely enough, Emma continued, that it was only the saps who hung around Cue.

'Oh?' said Linda, looking from Emma to Natasha with bewilderment.

'Did she?' Natasha asked, returning Linda's look with one of equal wonder.

'Well maybe it used to be like that or something, but it's not like that now. Not since we started going there, anyway.'

'Yeah, that's probably it,' said Emma, agreeing just a little too profoundly. They picked up on it, and having finished eating, left, saying that they had to go and finish some homework in the cloakrooms.

'Fucking eejits', said Emma. 'They're not mad at all, they're just poseurs who think they're mad.'

Linda and Natasha ceased paying her any attention whatsoever. Emma's eyes, however, continued to stray

23

towards them when they talked together at the back of the class, when she saw them during the break with their gang of about five girls from the other classes and occasionally Nuala and Nora from our class, and when she saw the gang setting off after school together, minus Nuala and Nora, on the way for a smoke up their lane. This was a practice the class was loudly informed of at the end of every day, as if the rest of us were not aware of it, although we had often enough seen it with our own eyes. Emma asked me about those other girls, but I wasn't much help to her as I didn't know them personally either. Our school was like that, you generally didn't know the people in the other classes in your year, not to mention anyone in the other years, as all the classes tended to keep to themselves. The only thing I could say was that they were probably exactly the same as Linda and Natasha.

'Do you think?' she had asked with uncertain speculation.

'Yes, I do,' I'd assured her, and the subject was dropped.

Emma's first week ended uneventfully, but she arrived in school the following Monday rejuvenated from a great night's drinking on the Saturday.

Everyone in school was talking about the Ashford disco. The Ashford disco was held once a fortnight in the Community Centre during the school year and was starting up again this coming Friday night, and it was going to be a particularly good one as it would be the first of the year. Apparently it had been getting quite rough towards the end of last year, but the troublemakers had all been barred, so it would be safe enough. Emma lost interest

24

after hearing that. A lot of the class were planning to go. I told her that I had gone once last year with Aisling. The music had been extremely loud and bad. They claimed to play a mixture of music, but in fact played a lot of poppy stuff and rave. The people who went there were our age group, from the school, and from similar schools in the area. We had left early. Emma laughed and said she could imagine.

This was at lunchtime, and we were walking around the grounds. She told me that the only disco in Kilmore was held once a month and was a bit like that. Nobody went because they were real strict and wouldn't let you in if you were pissed. And it was impossible to sneak drink in.

'So, you never go to discos then,' I said.

'No. Well, some of my friends go to raves in town and stuff, but I hate rave so I don't.'

'Do they drop Es and stuff?'

'No. Well, friends of friends do, but my friends don't.'

I was relieved. I wasn't up to dealing with drugs.

'They just smoke the odd bit of blow, like me.'

I hadn't been expecting this.

She looked at me and laughed. 'Chill out, Cassandra. The slightest thing and you're scandalised. Anyone who didn't know you'd swear you were real prim and proper, like my mam says I should be. Hash is nothing. It's like smoking, only you get a much better buzz, like you're locked out of your head on about twenty cans. It's not even addictive. It's not like getting stoned on heroin or anything.'

I did know it was a soft drug with only a psychological addiction, but I still didn't like the idea of it. To me, drugs were drugs, no matter what they were, and I told Emma so, at the risk of my reputation. She got annoyed at that.

'It's none of your business what I do with my body. I'd prefer to have a bit of fun and die young than be a dry-arse and live to be a hundred like you.'

I apologised and said I didn't mean it like that. And I didn't. Emma's approval meant a lot to me. I was just worried about her doing damage to herself, and I told her so. My concern pleased her, and she told me not to worry, she wasn't exactly stupid, and stayed well away from all the dangerous stuff.

We turned a corner, and saw Linda and Natasha walking in front of us. Emma motioned me to be quiet. I was delighted to drop the subject, as I felt my inadequacy was heightened by my inexperience and Emma's touchiness.

Natasha was talking about Gary, surprise, surprise. He hadn't been around Cue lately because he was hanging around with a new crowd. She mentioned some male names which made Emma look surprised and impressed. They were going to the disco, so Linda and Natasha were going too.

When they were out of earshot, Emma told me that she had heard of the fellas they were talking about from Michelle. She was always on about them. They were all mad and meant to be fucking rides. She wouldn't mind going to the disco just to have a look at them, and while she was there she might even get to meet Linda and Natasha's friends from school. Not that she cared about that or anything, she just wanted to know for certain that they were as bad as the other two. I thought that might not be a bad idea. Besides, she continued, her mam would be so happy if she went to a posh disco with the class. She was always on at her to 'settle in' and make friends. She'd been a pain in the arse all weekend telling her to study, but this might just loosen her up a bit. She'd only go if I went, though.

'You have to go,' she pleaded. 'There's no way I'm going on my own or with any of them.'

I agreed, happy at the prospect of a night out with Emma so soon, even if it was only to the Ashford disco.

'Oh my God, I've just thought,' Emma soon said. 'I've no way of getting home, unless I scrounge a lift off my da. Oh well, I suppose I'll have to do that so.'

'Why don't you stay in my house,' I suggested. 'That'd be the simplest thing for you to do.'

She thought about it. 'I suppose it would be,' she agreed casually. 'Will your parents mind?'

'No they won't,' I told her, and it was settled.

'And we'll finally get to see this Gary in the flesh. Wouldn't it be a sickener if he was a total dog?' Emma asked, and we laughed at the thought as we headed for the next class.

My parents said they couldn't wait to meet Emma and were glad to see me making an effort to mix with the class.

'My mam said not to get my hopes up, but I knew it'd be alright,' Emma said.

On Wednesday, I had a chat with Sinéad and Tessa, and was surprised when I thought that it was the first time I'd been talking to them properly since the first day, even though they sat in front of us. I supposed it had something

27

to do with the fact that they didn't like Emma, which made our little talk quite awkward. I just asked them were they going to the disco, and they said no, they hadn't liked it last year and they couldn't imagine it being any different this time around. I said I was just going because Emma wanted to see what it was like and she would be staying in my house. They said that was nice, and we left it at that.

I was feeling relatively confident about Friday night. Emma had asked me if there was any way we could get drink and I had told her it was impossible in Ashford, and even if we got some we would definitely be snared. Thankfully that had been sufficient and she had asked no more questions. She would come home with me after school on Friday, help me pick out what to wear and help me with my hair and make-up. It would be a good night anyway, even if the disco was bad.

CHAPTER 4

On Friday evening, after Emma's daily smoke – with one extra as a special treat for making it to the end of the school week – we went on to my house. She was laden down with bags although I had relieved her of her school bag: she had brought with her a selection of outfits to choose from, her wine Docs, make-up, hairspray and pyjamas.

'I like to do things with style,' she told me when I asked if that mountain of stuff was really necessary. 'Anyway, I got a lift to school with me da and Brenda's going to meet me off the bus tomorrow, so I'll be grand.'

We reached my road just as I was beginning to think that my arms were going to fall off and roll down the road with Emma's graffitoed books, many of which read prominently 'EMMA AND PAUL' or 'BRENDA LUVS TOMO 4 EVER'. Tomo was the fella Brenda was meeting at the moment. In Kilmore, 'meeting' someone meant getting off with them but not going out with them (yet). Emma said that the meaning often varied from town to town. Paul was the ride that everyone, including Emma, was mad into; he was eighteen, in a band, and lived on Michelle's estate which was one of the two council estates in Kilmore. There were loads of other estates in Kilmore, but there was very little council housing. Some of the best-looking fellas lived on Michelle's estate, which was a problem, because there were also a lot of what Emma's mam called 'troublemakers' living there – so she didn't like Emma going down there at night. In fact, she didn't let Emma go up to Kilmore Village on her own at night because there were plenty of troublemakers from the rest of Kilmore and you never knew what might happen, even though the village was more brightly lit and most people were decent.

'My mam's like that,' Emma had said. 'She's so paranoid.'

My own mother had told me that most of the houses out there were very small, like where we used to live. I remembered our old house being small.

I pointed out my house from the top of the road. Emma was astounded at how big it was, especially for just three people. When we got there she started to climb the steps to the door facing the street, but I told her to come through the other door.

'Two front doors! Very posh.'

She followed me through to the kitchen where my dad was cooking dinner. My mum came in from the sitting room when she heard us and the introductions were made.

'The dinner'll be ready in about two minutes so you might as well sit down now,' my dad said, so we sat at the table with my mum. Emma was very quiet, only speaking when spoken to by either parent, who asked about school and her own parents, and so on. After dinner, I showed her the rest of the house on the way up to my room, and she said that her whole house would fit into my dad's study alone.

She loved my room. After depositing her bags on the bed, she walked around, looked out the window, and stared with disgust at her own reflection in the mirrors, and started to rearrange her hair.

'This is a deadly room,' she said. 'I'd do anything for a room like this.'

'Do you like the way it's done up?' I asked, pleased.

'Oh, yeah, it's perfect, only I'd have some posters on the wall. I have these posters of Keanu Reeves and Slash out of Guns 'n' Roses on the wall opposite my bed so that I can see them every morning when I wake up,' she laughed.

'I hate posters, though. They always end up ripping and falling off the walls.'

'So what? All you have to do is buy new ones. You can afford it,' she answered, with a touch of coldness.

Comments about how much better off I was than her made me feel uncomfortable. It was what I had most hoped to avoid. Just as well Emma put on a Metallica tape, turned it up loud and sung along to bits of it; the sound drowned out any awkward silences.

Emma unpacked her clothes and laid them out on the bed. She had a long, wide, red crushed-velvet skirt she'd got for Christmas, a pair of black stretch jeans, a black body top, a long black indian shirt with tassles, and a shorter, purple one, high stiletto-heeled black suede ankle boots, and of course, the love of her life, her black biker jacket. She had bought it second-hand with her birthday money and had paid a lot extra as it was painted all over with white, purple and red roses, entangled in thorny green stems. It was quite old, with a few rips and fading paint, which made it even nicer, Emma said. Everyone wanted her jacket, but she refused to sell it.

'What are you wearing tonight?' Emma asked me, as she started putting in her ear-studs at the mantlepiece mirror.

'You have to help me decide,' I said, going to the wardrobe and taking out a long plain white shirt, a black suede waistcoat, a long black indian skirt, fringed like Emma's shirts, and a pair of black leggings.

'This is all the stuff I have that fits me properly, apart from two pairs of jeans and a lumberjack shirt,' I said, remembering tales of Emma's vast wardrobe. 'I grew over the summer. I used to be tiny, no, well, that's an exaggeration, but I used to be a bit smaller than everyone else in school and now I'm taller than them, except for you that is.'

Emma was about a head taller than me and looked a lot older than she really was, which was fourteen going on fifteen. Her birthday was just before Christmas, and that pissed her off because she said she didn't get as many presents as she would have if her birthday was in June, say, like mine.

She examined the clothes critically. 'I've an idea. Do you have a black body top?' she asked, and I told her I did.

'Well then, why don't you wear my purple shirt over it and your black skirt?'

I was delighted. It was a gorgeous shirt, even though it was very loose on me when I tried it on. But it looked better when I pulled the neck right down, rolled up the sleeves, and put on the only jewellery I had, a silver cross which hung from a long stretch of black string.

'That shirt nearly looks better on you than it does on me,' Emma said, sounding almost surprised. 'I'm going to wear my red velvet skirt. Could I borrow your waistcoat if it fits me?'

'Of course you can.' I was delighted to lend her something. 'And it should fit you. It's quite a big one, and you can let it out at the back.'

She changed quickly and put the waistcoat on over her body top, loosening the back as far as it would go, and doing up the buttons.

'This looks deadly,' she said. It fitted her, but only just. Emma wasn't just taller than me, she had a broader build as well, but she insisted it wasn't too tight, and so the question of clothes was settled.

It was now six o'clock, which gave us plenty of time, Emma said, to do our hair and make-up. She put moisturiser on my face and then I went down to the kitchen to get us some coffee and biscuits. While we were eating, she stared appraisingly at me.

'I'm trying to decide what kind of hairstyle and make-up would suit you,' she explained.

I was pleased by all this attention as it made me feel important. She continued to scrutinise me, my skinniness, my long, blonde hair, and my grey eyes. So intensely, that I began to feel edgy and uncomfortable and was relieved when she spoke.

'What sort of make-up do you have?'

I showed her the powder foundation I had in the shade that matched my skin colour and the soft brown eyeliner pencil. She rubbed some of the foundation on my hand and frowned.

'You'd look like the walking dead with that on. I don't mean to be bad or anything, but friends have to be honest about these things.'

She took out her own, which was the same kind of make-up but darker, too dark for me. We both burst out laughing when we saw it.

'What would suit you best would be a darker shade than the one you have, though, so keep that in mind the next time you're in town or somewhere and have the time to mess around and pick out one that suits,' she said. 'Just do your own the way you always do, for now, anyway.'

I piled it on with increasing confidence. When I'd bought it, the salesgirl had said it might be too heavy for my skin, but that was what I loved about it. It blocked out everything completely, spots, pimples and oily patches. All of them. It made me feel passably presentable, and once out of the house and away from any mirrors the tight feeling on my skin reassured me that it was still there. Emma was the same. She wore it to school even. I didn't, because my skin dried out and went all flaky if I wore it too often so I had to ration it, and even though I rarely went anywhere else, I felt it was too good to be wasted on school. It was looking good tonight.

When I was finished, I turned to Emma. She examined me, and told me to wipe away the eyeliner.

'Your eyes are big enough, they don't need to be brought out any further.'

I did as she said, but then I thought it looked better the other way because I looked very plain and bland with no make-up at all on my eyes, and I didn't use that much

34

anyway, so I put it back the way it was, even though Emma didn't agree.

She put on her own make-up, the dark shade called 'Tanned Beige', or something, thick blue eyeliner, and red lipstick. Then she brushed her hair out, took her mousse, and scrunched some in to make her hair wavier and thicker. I watched her with fascination as I had never been able to make that stuff work on my hair, and she seemed to be doing a good job even though she was using up a lot of it. She took out her hairspray, backcombed the front of her hair away from her face and sprayed it thoroughly, releasing strong, sweet fumes which sickened me for a few moments. Then she pinned the doctored areas carefully against her head.

'This is to hold it in place while it dries,' she explained. 'You can dry it with a hairdryer, only that makes it go hard and sticky. It's much better this way.'

She put her little silver stud in her nose and began to put on her vast heap of jewellery. She looked amazing. No wonder it took her so long to get ready.

'Do you want me to do your hair now?' she asked, fastening the clasp on the final choker.

'Whenever you're ready,' I said, brushing the knots out of it.

'I'm ready now.' She picked up her cans of hairspray and mousse, removed the bangles from her arms, sat me on my chair, and after a cursory brushing began to backbrush it gently and scrunch it up with mousse, as she had one with her own. When that was done to her satisfaction, she treated the front of it as she had done her own, pinned it back, and told me not to move or touch it until it had set.

35

Returning to her spot in front of the mirror, she carefully took her hair down, assessed it, and gave it a final generous all-over spray.

'What do you think?' she asked, turning to face me.

She looked even better than I had imagined she would.

'You look deadly,' I said, adopting one of her favourite words.

She smiled and swung back to the mirror for another look. 'It'll do, I suppose.'

She then took down my hair, fluffed it up, and dragged me to the mirror, delighted with her work. I touched it as I examined it. Up close, the front looked wet and shiny like Emma's, only it felt hard and slimy to my fingers, and the rest of it felt papery. But I liked it. It was the way I had always wanted it. Finally seeing it made me feel older, and more like how a friend of Emma's should look.

'It's gorgeous. You'll have to show me how to do it myself.'

'It's real easy, all you need is the right kind of mousse and hairspray.' She was pleased and handed me the cans. I examined them and committed the brand names to memory so that I could buy some for myself.

Emma returned her bangles to her arms, noticing as she did the time on her watch.

'It's getting late, we'd better head.'

She reached for her jacket and counted her money.

'Shit, I'm going to have to buy smokes on the way and I don't have enough dosh. Can you lend me two pounds and I'll pay you back on Monday?'

I took down my jacket from its hook. It was nothing compared to Emma's but it was nice enough. It was a jet black jacket in the same denim as the jeans Emma had brought over. I opened the pocket where I had put the five-pound note my parents had given me for tonight plus another fiver in loose change. I counted out two pounds which Emma put with her smokes money which she then zipped into a separate pocket. Into another pocket went her make-up, and she put her comb into the large inside pocket.

'Do you always bring all that with you?' I asked, curious.

'Most of the time, yeah, in case I need it.'

She put her jacket on in front of the mirror and shook her hair out. I quietly slipped my own make-up into a pocket with my front-door key; Emma knew best, she was more used to going out than I was, although I felt any nerves I had about tonight disappear as I gave myself a final glance in the mirror and saw my hair again and how good Emma's shirt looked with my skirt. Then I followed an impatient Emma out the door, turning the light off and firmly closing the door to conserve the heat in my room on this beautiful, clear and crisp, but chilly night in mid September.

We quickly said goodbye to my parents who told us both that we looked very nice and to have a good time, and then we left, shivering as we pulled the front door behind us. It was half-seven and not dark yet, but the light was dimming and the street lamps were lit, and seeing them, Emma said, always put her in a good mood for a night out, no matter where she was going.

We soon arrived at a shop where Emma bought an extravagant pack of twenty smokes, and lit one up as soon as we'd left the relative brightness and bustle of the village behind. I had got used to her smoking and I didn't mind the pollution any more. I had also stopped looking over my shoulder every time she had a cigarette in her mouth in case a teacher or someone we knew saw us.

CHAPTER 5

Ten minutes and two cigarettes later we reached the Community Centre, which was basically a large gym hall complete with coloured tracks painted on the wooden floor and basketball nets. There was a small crowd ahead of us but we saw no-one we knew as we waited our turn to pay the three-pound entrance fee to the sound of The Doors playing 'Light My Fire'. Emma grabbed my arm with delight, told me this was her all-time favourite song, and sung it as we walked into the darkened hall.

She surveyed the hall with its temporary DJ and lighting set up at the top and benches arranged against the walls and shouted to me that the disco in Kilmore was like this. They started playing some rave song and we made faces of disgust at each other.

'This is what I hate about these things, having to listen to shit music at full volume,' I shouted.

'I know. Let's go for a walk and see who's here.'

We walked around the rapidly filling hall. There were a lot of people up dancing, others standing around talking. Emma remarked that none of them were up to much. They were mainly people of our age from the local schools, although some of them would be from other areas and would have got buses over here, and some of them were quite ravery, although not real ravers like the ones Emma knew.

We saw some girls from school whom we decided to avoid. Then we noticed Linda and Natasha in their raver gear sitting looking dazed on a corner bench. We decided to go over and say hello as we were keen to have the famous Gary and Michelle's beloved lads from Crossgrange pointed out to us. Natasha sat staring over our heads into space.

Linda stood up and fell onto Emma as she gave her a hug. 'Hello, Emma, I'm pissed,' she said in an imbecilic voice and fell back onto her seat.

The sudden jerk seemed to wake Natasha. 'Hello everybody,' she said, waving her arm in wide unbalanced movements, and almost knocking over someone passing by. 'You two look nice tonight.'

'Thanks,' said Emma, sitting on the bench at the adjacent wall. I sat down beside her. Their enthusiastic welcome surprised me, but then this was probably standard drunken behaviour.

'Where did youse get the drink?' Emma asked.

Natasha smiled in triumphant recollection. 'Linda took two cans of beer from her house and brought them over to my house because my parents were going out and we drank them there.'

'I see,' Emma said. 'Oh, my God, they're so sad,' she whispered in my ear. 'Imagine getting drunk on one can each.'

'Is your ex here tonight?' she asked.

Natasha jumped up, took Emma's arm and led her to

the other side of the hall, while Emma beckoned me to follow them.

'There he is with the new crowd he's hanging around with,' Natasha said proudly, and we found ourselves gazing upon a scrawny little midget amidst a gang of equally unattractive ravers.

'Very nice,' said Emma, as we looked at each other with disgust. We went back to Linda who was now surrounded by what we called the smoking gang. We talked to them for a little while before leaving, saying vaguely that we'd see them later.

'They're as sad as everyone else in school,' Emma said as soon as we were out of earshot. The speakers continued to belt out non-stop rave.

'And I swear to God if I have to listen to rave and snobby voices for much longer I'll go mad! I don't mean you though, yours doesn't wreck the head like theirs do.'

I thanked her for the compliment. I didn't have a 'snobby accent', but I didn't have a Dublin accent either. In fact I talked like Emma did when she was in school – she always used her polite voice which she said was how her mam talked, though she had more of a Dublin accent outside school and when she was with me.

We sat down together on a bench from which Gary and the others could be watched. 'He is such a dog,' said Emma looking over at him. 'This place is pissing me off.'

I agreed with her, and we sat for a few minutes without speaking as the so-called music did not make it easy to talk.

One of Gary's friends walked slowly in our direction, and stopped in front of us. 'Alright,' he said, taking long slow drags out of his cigarette.

Me and Emma looked at each other with surprise. 'Hi,' we said together.

'I'm eh, I'm Dave, by the way. Listen, there's a mate of mine that's mad into you,' he said, looking directly at me.

'Me?' I asked.

I looked at Emma and we burst out laughing.

'Go on then, point him out to us,' Emma said, and our laughter intensified when we saw that he meant Gary himself.

'Well?' Emma asked me when we'd quietened down.

'No,' I said firmly.

'Fair enough. There's your answer,' she said to Dave, who slunk back to his friends.

'He must think we're mad,' I said, slightly ashamed of our unsubtlety.

'We are mad, in the good sense,' Emma said. 'But we'd have to be mad in the worst sense to even think for you to go near your man, fucking scummy or what.'

I was thrilled to hear Emma rank me with herself. It made me feel good, although my head was beginning to split with all the noise and my throat to tighten in the smoky atmosphere.

'What's the matter?'

'All this bad music is going to my head.'

'Do you want to go then? I'm bored, you're bored, and you've got a headache, so it's really not worth our while hanging around.'

It was the best thing I could have hoped for.

As we made our way out, we came across Natasha wandering around distractedly.

'Where are you two off to?'

'Home,' I said.

'Home,' she echoed looking at her watch. 'At this hour?'

'Yeah, we're sick of listening to rave,' Emma explained.

Natasha looked us up and down. 'Not your style is it? Oh, well, suit yourselves.

'I saw you talking to Dave earlier.' She looked at us questioningly. Emma smiled at me and neither of us spoke. I didn't know what to do or say and stared at Emma in confusion, appealing for guidance, unable to read any signs in her face, transfigured by the bright flashing lights bouncing on and off her.

'So what was he saying, go on, tell me,' Natasha asked with growing persistence.

'Tell her, Cassandra.'

'No, you can tell her.'

If anyone was going to tell her it would be Emma. I wouldn't know what to say.

'Alright then, if you're sure you really want to know,' Emma said to Natasha.

Her face lit up with anticipation while Emma savoured the suspense, before continuing.

'He was asking Cassandra if she'd meet that fella, Gary you're always going on about.'

She spoke in a gentle and reluctant tone; this was, after all, the love of Natasha's life, even if neither of them were up to much.

'Yeah? What d'you say?' Natasha asked, looking at me strangely. I was surprised to read contempt and dislike in her eyes, but I told myself that she must be upset and

43

hoped it was an illusion created by the lights, which distorted everybody's features.

'I said no,' I told her, hoping that would diminish her antipathy towards me, but it didn't. She said something which I couldn't make out over the noise.

'Sorry, what?' I asked.

'I see,' she said, loud and hard.

I felt very awkward and looked at Emma for guidance. Emma took my arm firmly and looked dismissively at Natasha. 'I told her she was dead right too, not wanting to go near a dog like that. Anyway, we're going now. Bye.'

She steered me well away from Natasha and out of the disco. 'Silly bitch,' Emma said. 'Don't worry about it.'

'What was her problem?' I asked.

Emma shrugged her shoulders. 'God only knows. She's probably just jealous that he wanted you instead of her.'

'You shouldn't have said he was a dog, that'll only make things worse.'

'So what? It served her right. You shouldn't take any shit from young ones like that.'

'But I still have to see her every day in school.'

'That doesn't mean you have to talk to her.'

'I suppose,' I said, wanting the subject to go away.

We walked back to my house, Emma chattering away about nothing of great importance or interest, and me saying nothing at all apart from vague acknowledgements of her statements. We went into the kitchen and talked for about five minutes to my parents about how boring the disco was before escaping up to my room with coffee and food. I could see that Emma was still not really comfortable talking to them and didn't want to hang around. I was

44

still upset about Natasha but did not want to discuss it with them as I felt that they would more than likely tell me I was paranoid and over-reacting, as she hadn't actually *said* anything to me, and that it wasn't my fault anyway, so I shouldn't get all worked up about it.

'Stop thinking about her,' Emma ordered me as soon as we were settled upstairs, me in my armchair pulled over to the bed where Emma lay and the tray on the chair borrowed from my desk placed at mutual arm's reach.

'Because if you don't, you'll be depressed all the time, and the night will be ruined.'

I smiled sadly and Emma rolled her eyes. 'Cheer up! Believe me, anyone who gets pissed on one can and gives you grief over some sap is not worth bothering about. It makes you almost as sad as she is. So let's talk about something nice, like you coming drinking with me in Kilmore next weekend.'

'That'd be deadly,' I said wistfully, acknowledging to myself that it would be wasted on me as I would probably mess up completely out of nerves and ignorance of how to behave and make a fool of myself, and of Emma as well, for having the bad sense to bring me along. The incident with Natasha had shaken me. Why the dislike of someone I disliked myself affected me so much, I didn't understand, and that confusion intensified my low spirits.

'Don't look so happy about it. I thought you wanted to come out with me and meet all my friends.'

I saw that I had upset and insulted her. 'That's not it at all, you've got the wrong idea.'

She still looked at me suspiciously and I didn't blame her, as I probably looked as unenthusiastic and depressed as

45

I sounded, and Emma couldn't possibly realise what was going on in my head. I had led her to believe that I was equal to her in experience and behaviour through insinuating silences which were almost as effective as direct lies. I didn't know what to say to her, nor she, it would appear, to me, as she was now staring at me in puzzlement and bemusement.

'Is it safe for me to have a smoke out the window? The wind'll blow the smell away and I'll spray some deodorant around the room.'

I looked at the clock. 'My parents'll be watching their video, but still, are you sure you should risk it? We'd be killed.'

'Stop shitting bricks, will you. They won't come up. Anyway, I'm an expert, I do this all the time in my gaff and Brenda's.'

She seemed irritated, so I agreed. She turned the light off so no one outside could see, half-opened the window and lit up a smoke, holding it out the window, the curtains closed behind her and blowing in the wind. I was relieved to smell very little cigarette smoke, and that the house wasn't visible from the back. But I was shaking with fear in case they came upstairs early and flinched at the slightest sounds: Emma moving her feet or the wind blowing.

'You're upset about something, aren't you?' Emma said sympathetically from the window. Both her accuracy and the sound of her voice almost made me jump out of my skin.

'Now, don't deny it, because I can tell. Do you want to talk about it? I might be able to help.'

I knew very well she could help, but I wasn't sure that

she'd want to, and I liked her too much to want to ruin my standing in her eyes. I was afraid to confide in her, and ashamed of myself for not trusting her, but I had never been able to trust other girls. Even with Aisling there were things I never told her.

'I don't know how to say it,' I said, stalling for time.

'Just think it over,' she encouraged. 'Come over here and look out, it's deadly.'

I knelt beside her, draping the curtains behind us and leaning my elbows on the window sill. The wind blew my hair back from my face, soothing and cooling my hot flushed cheeks and forehead. The light over the back door had been left on, casting the garden and conservatory into shadow, conspiring with the wind in the trees of our garden, and the majestic older ones beyond. In the distance was the sound of traffic.

'This is deadly,' I parroted.

Emma smiled. 'It's like something out of a horror film. There'd better not be any vampires and werewolves waiting to hop on us.'

'Don't say things like that. I have to live here.'

Emma picked up her cigarettes and lit up another one. 'A lot of people I know who don't smoke always have a cigarette when they're upset or depressed. They say it makes them feel better. Do you want one?'

I didn't think it was such a good idea as once me and Aisling had tried one and put it aside in disgust after a tiny puff each, but I could see that Emma genuinely thought it could help and I didn't want to offend her, so I agreed hesitantly.

She lit one off the end of her own and handed it to me,

47

one drag down, tip glowing fire-red in the darkness. I stiffened my face so that it would show no reaction and inhaled slowly, gently, warily and cautiously. It was like standing beside a smoking peat fire and taking huge gulps. That was all. Unpleasant, stifling and throat parching, but bearable. I exhaled and inhaled again with Emma's encouragement, and again. I was getting light-headed and nauseous but there wasn't much left to go so I decided to finish it off in one fell swoop and took a long deep drag, like Emma's post-withdrawal ones. The nausea rose as I choked and coughed, my throat burned, my lungs felt suffocated and drowned inside my chest.

I lay on my bed to weather the storm as Emma frantically stubbed out both cigarettes in a cascade of flying sparks, shut the window, closed the curtains, turned the lights on, ran around the room spraying deodorant, and stood at the door listening for my parents, who to both our relief stayed downstairs, presumably still watching their video.

I was left drained and with a bad taste in my mouth. Emma got me a drink of water from the bathroom in my empty coffee cup which I drank in two long swallows. It was lukewarm and stale, and tasted faintly of coffee, but it revived me slightly. The deodorant in the air sickened me, but it was gradually fading away. I put the cup down and looked at her in embarrassment.

'Was that your first cigarette?'

I nodded.

'Don't worry about it. Loads of people get sick first time round.'

I realised that I was about to cry, but before I could

suppress the urge, Emma gave me a big hug and asked me what else was wrong – it wasn't just that – and she wanted to know what it was, and the tears came pouring out. I didn't think I could tell her, but I saw by looking at her that she really was worried and concerned and that gave me courage. I told myself that I'd already made a fool of myself so things couldn't get any worse.

'I'm not what you think I am, Emma. I'd kill to be like you, but I'm not. I can't go out with you, because I'd make a fool of myself. I've never been drinking in my life, so I wouldn't know what to do. I'd just make you look stupid for bringing me. The only times I ever drank alcohol were whenever me and Aisling robbed some wine or beer at Christmas or whenever our parents had parties. And the only time I ever had a smoke was when me and Aisling took one of her mum's and one little puff made me feel sick so I put it out, and you've just seen what one cigarette did to me, so you can imagine what some blow would do to me. And I've never got off with a fella either, so you see, I'm probably as bad as everyone else in school only worse, because at least they've got each other and their poxy fellas, and I have no one now that Aisling's gone.'

I was relieved to have set Emma straight, but I felt so desolate because my standing in her eyes had now been destroyed completely. As I thought over what I had said, I became sure she wouldn't want me hanging around with her outside school anymore and I burst into tears again. I quickly subdued them and rubbed and pulled harshly at the skin around my eyes, mortified and ashamed of myself.

'Don't worry about it, it doesn't matter,' Emma said.

'And what do you mean you've no friends? You've got me, haven't you?'

So we were still friends. That was the best thing I could have heard.

'Yes, I do,' I said more cheerfully, wiping my eyes and blowing my nose in tissues that disintegrated on touching my face.

'And you're not that far behind us, you know. We're only going out drinking properly since the beginning of the summer. Before that it was occasional. And we still stroke drink on the oul pair when we can get it. We're not made of money you know,' she laughed.

I finished blowing my nose and looked with horror in the mirror. My eyes were all red and sunken in a setting of equally red and swollen flesh. My make-up had disintegrated into a mess of runny streaks and flaky pieces, some of which had dried into the flushed pores. I looked disgusting.

'I think I'd better wash my face right now,' I said.

'I think that'd be a good idea,' she answered, and we both smiled at each other.

Heart lightened, I went to the bathroom and went to the toilet, I'd been dying to go for ages. I washed my teeth thoroughly, and my face with doubled care. Body restored, I opened the door to see Emma standing there barefoot, in a blue nightie with 'Sweet Dreams' written all over in pink, and clutching a cosmetic bag. She took her turn in the bathroom while I changed and went down to say good night to my parents who said they were on their way up. I returned to find Emma tucked up in bed, turned off the main light, and knocked on the lamp beside my bed (because we weren't going to sleep yet, we were still going to talk, Emma said) and climbed into bed.

'Are you still coming out with us, then?'

'I'd love to, if it's alright.'

'Of course it is. I won't be able to drink that much anyway, because, my mam is beginning to cop that I drink, so I have to be careful. It'll be alright, though, I'll just knock back a few cans as soon as we're out to get a buzz, and I'll be sober by the time we go back. That'll do me. What about you, though? How much can you take? I don't want you getting sick, or coming back to my gaff locked.'

'Me and Aisling used to take two cans each, or half a bottle of wine between us. And that'd have us buzzing for the night, only it'd wear right down after a couple of hours, so we could let on we were normal.'

'And did youse drink in your gaffs?'

'Yeah, we'd keep it till our parents had gone out for the night and drink it then. Only about once a year, though.'

'I don't know about wine, but two cans'd be grand for you, but you'd have to leave it if it was getting too much for you, because I don't want you snared rapid, right?'

'Whatever you say, you know best. Where'll we go?'

'It depends. We'll go wherever we're least likely to be snared by the pigs.'

'The police? What happens if they catch us? Do they arrest us, or what?' The idea of police was very unsettling. It had somehow never occurred to me. Parents had, irate neighbours, and nosey passers-by, but not police. Emma was breaking her arse laughing. 'Fucking eejit. Of course they won't arrest us. They'll just shove us in their car and bring us home. Bad, but not that bad. Arrest us.' She laughed derisively and I felt stupid.

'Well, in America they do. You see it on the telly all the time.'

'That's just on the telly though. Besides, the pigs over there are completely off their heads.'

'No, I'm positive they do. In some states they'll arrest you for anything.' But I was no longer so sure of myself. I'd write to Aisling and find out. I'd only had one short letter from her ages ago in which she'd promised to write properly soon. I'd wait till I'd heard from her.

'Who else'll be there?'

'Oh, everyone. All my friends, ones from my old school, loads of fellas. And we'll have to set you up with someone. Me and Brenda'll have to have a think about that one. Someone nice.'

The thought of it filled me with fear, but I wanted to get it over with so that I could truthfully say I'd been with someone. 'You'll make sure it's someone nice, won't you? I'll be real nervous, Emma. I hope I won't fuck up.'

'No, you won't be actually fucking the man, just getting off with him,' she assured me jocularly, and laughed, while I felt myself turn a bright red.

'You know what I mean though.'

'Of course I do. Don't worry about it. It'll come naturally to you and he'll never know the difference. We'll make sure it's someone who's a bit shy, so he won't try anything on you.'

'What's he likely to try?'

'You'd be surprised. All fellas are randy perverts, and sometimes the quiet ones are the worst of all. They'll be feeling your arse and your tits, and the next thing you know, they'll be trying to finger you in broad daylight with everyone looking. But don't you worry. I'll see you right. Stop looking so nervous.'

'Have you gone out with many fellas?'

'I suppose you could say that. I'm not a slut or anything, but compared to Brenda, now, I've had a good few. Brenda's not very good-looking, you see, and a lot of fellas are real shallow so they won't go near her.'

'Did you ever have sex with anyone?'

'I've done everything but, but I've never actually shagged anyone. I know some people who have, but I want to wait till I meet the right person, and I don't care how young or old I am.'

'Would you not be afraid of getting pregnant?'

'No. Not as long as I was using a condom.'

'They're not a hundred per cent, though, and they tear.'

'They're 95 or 97, or something like that, and that's good enough for me. Besides, if they tear you can get the morning-after. Or I might just take the Pill. Anyway, it doesn't matter, because I haven't got my eye on anyone at the moment.'

'So you won't be meeting anyone on Saturday night then.'

'No, and it's just as well, because I'll be in me flowers, and I hate meeting anyone then.'

'You'll be what?'

'Periods. Once a month like clockwork, unlike Brenda, who never knows when they'll come. What about you?'

'Regular enough, I suppose, about once every six

weeks, but I've only been getting them since just before the summer, so . . .'

'So you don't really know what the story is. You'll know only too well in a while, though. Believe me. What time is it? Oh my God, we'd better get some sleep. Turn out the light, will you?'

I did, but I was restless and my head was spinning and turning over the events of the evening time and time again, and I couldn't sleep. Neither could Emma, because about twenty minutes later, she asked me was I still awake, and we stayed up talking for hours until she dropped off much later. We talked about anything and everything, and before the night was out, I knew exactly where to go to get clothes like Emma's, and I lay awake planning what I was going to buy to the sound of her snores.

We woke at about half-twelve the following morning. Emma rushed off without breakfast in a panic because she was late home, and her mam would kill her. I ran to the bus stop with her and walked slowly back, still exhausted, but much happier and less anxious about Emma and the future. My mother told me that Emma seemed like a nice girl, only did her mother approve of her walking around with nose rings and earrings all over her.

'No, but she can't do anything about it because they've arrangements and deals about all these things,' I answered.

'I see,' she said.

She said I could spend the night at Emma's next Saturday night, providing I put the spare bed back into the spare room, and I went upstairs, glad to have that sorted out. I saw my waistcoat folded on the back of the chair, and went to put it away. When I opened it out, I saw that the inside seams underneath the armpits were burst, and the suede around the tits part of it was all stretched and pulled out of shape. It was ruined and there was nothing I could do about it. I couldn't put it in the wash, and dry-cleaning wouldn't make much difference. It looked just as bad on, because Emma had much bigger tits than me. My beautiful waistcoat. I knew she hadn't meant to do it and I wasn't going to mention it to her, but that cloud dampened my spirits and hung over me for the rest of the day.

CHAPTER 6

I was at school ten minutes early the following Monday. Neither Emma nor Linda nor Natasha were in sight and when I walked into the classroom some of the girls became silent and looked at me furtively. Áine, who was sitting on a desk nearby, turned to face me.

'Did Gary really ask you up at the disco on Friday night?' she asked.

'Yeah,' I answered, wondering what she was getting at. Everyone had been listening, and they all laughed slyly and meaningfully to themselves and each other.

'And I said no,' I added.

'And did you tell Natasha about it before you left?' someone else asked.

'No, well, I didn't but Emma did.'

Everyone laughed gleefully and with mock rebuke. Then Áine said, 'It's a pity you left so early, you should have seen what happened next.' She paused for effect and the laughter resumed.

'Natasha was still pissed, and Gary went and asked her up. And she had an unopened can of Coke in her hand, and she'd been messing with it, throwing it up in the air and catching it, and stuff. Anyway, as soon as he asked her up, she started screaming at him. "You fucking prick, you

56

are such a sleaze," and stuff like that, and he said, "shut up, you stupid bitch," and turned to walk off – he didn't know what she was on about – and she shouted "don't you dare walk away from me, you fucking bastard," and opened her can and sprayed it right in his face, and it went in his eyes, and all over his hair and his clothes, and he looked such a state, all wet and sticky.'

I could imagine it alright and burst out laughing. 'He got what what was coming to him,' I said.

'He sure did,' someone said. 'Especially considering he was two-timing her with somebody else when he was going with her. But that didn't make any difference to her, she loved him anyway. At least now she's come to her senses.'

'Well, at least that much good has come of it,' Áine agreed. 'Poor Natasha was thrown out of the disco and barred from ever going back, and she always loved going there. She used to look forward to it every week. She won't forget this in a hurry.'

It was now almost ten-past nine, and the teacher rushed in, shutting us up. Her arrival coincided with that of Linda and Natasha. Natasha swaggered in and over to her desk, looking a bit embarrassed though defiant and taking care to catch no-one's eye except for one filthy look at me. I desperately willed Emma to come in, as I needed to discuss all this with her. I knew that no-one else in school blamed me for what had happened, but Natasha did, and I didn't know how to handle it.

I was glad to see Emma rushing past the window and into the classroom with profuse apologies. I wrote her a quick letter on the back page of a copy book, struggling to maintain an appearance of calm

'Fucking eejit,' Emma wrote back. 'Exactly what is to be expected from a low IQ Under the Influence.'

'But she blames me for it,' I whispered.

'So what. Fuck her, we can take it.'

I didn't get the opportunity to say anything else because the teacher told us to be quiet and kept a close eye on us for the rest of the class.

Linda and Natasha kept a lower-than-usual profile that day, and avoided and ignored me and Emma from then on. The class soon forgot about what had happened, or at least stopped talking about it, but I couldn't forget about it, as Natasha continued to give me dirty looks whenever we were within a hundred yards of each other. Emma would stare right back at her and tell me not to worry about it and to ignore her, she was just a stupid bitch, but after all, what else could you expect from this school?

'You have to stand up for yourself,' she said. 'You can't let young ones like that push you around.'

Although I couldn't forget about it, I at least stopped trying to understand Natasha's behaviour in my head. I concentrated on the good things that were happening in my life, like how much closer me and Emma were becoming, how even the class now grouped us together. It was always 'Emma and Cassandra', or 'Cassandra and Emma', which delighted me, and at times overawed me. We had reached this stage so soon.

We spent the breaks between classes talking; at little break and lunchtime, we would go off on our own somewhere. We had things to discuss. Emma and Brenda were still in the process of finding me a fella, and she'd had to tell Brenda that this would be my first one.

'You don't mind, do you?' she asked me anxiously. 'I had to tell her, so she'd know what to look for, but she won't say anything to anyone, she promised, and I know you don't know her, but she's my best friend, well you and her are, so you can trust her.'

My anguish over someone else knowing vanished at that. To think I was one of Emma's best friends!

'No, it's alright, just don't tell anyone else.'

'Of course I won't. What d'you think I am?'

She'd told Brenda all about me, and she was dying to meet me, so was half of Kilmore, and I was filled with both anticipation and dread of Saturday night. Anticipation of how wonderful it would be, and dread of making a fool of myself and discrediting myself completely in Emma's eyes. This fear had still remained, in spite of last Friday night and Emma's assurances to the contrary.

Above all, I was nervous about meeting Brenda. She had been Emma's best friend since they were little girls, and it was vital that she like me, because if she didn't, then that would be the end of friendship with Emma. She would still be friends with me in school because we sat beside each other and she didn't like anyone else, but I would never get to go to Kilmore again, and while simultaneously longing for and dreading Kilmore, the thought of having it swept permanently from under my feet was devastatingly awful. So I had to make a good impression on Brenda. At the very least, if I didn't make a fool of myself, she wouldn't have a chance to condemn me even if she didn't like me, and if everyone else liked me, then maybe she would give me a second chance and get to like me then. Brenda was important. She was Emma's Only Real Close Friend (apart from me, that is, she told me). Both of them had loads of other friends, but they were only people they hung around with and went drinking with in big gangs. They weren't people Emma and Brenda got close to otherwise, or trusted with their personal business. While being the maddest and the wildest of their set, they weren't close to any of the others, even though they got on very well with everyone else, especially the ones from Emma's old school, and helped anyone out that needed them.

The only possible exception was Michelle, but that was on an on-and-off basis, and it was a while since they'd got on really well with her and even then not as well as with each other. Emma didn't like her very much at the moment, although Brenda was sitting beside her and hanging around with her a bit in school now that Emma had gone. Michelle didn't live near them (she lived in the estate of rides), and most of her friends didn't go to Brenda's school, or as Emma put it, didn't go to school. Sometimes some of Michelle's friends hung around with Emma and Brenda's gang, and sometimes not. There was usually an open arrangement made to go drinking on a Friday or a Saturday night, and whoever wanted to go, or could go, went. And this weekend it would be a fairly large crowd going out on the Saturday night.

We had to plan out everything, what time I would come at – I was to come in the afternoon so that we'd have loads of time and Emma could show me around the place and I could meet Brenda and stuff. We talked so much in class that the teachers threatened us with separation. I loved every minute of it. We talked loudly about the great night ahead of us whenever anyone could hear, especially Linda and Natasha. Some of them were interested and envious. A good few from the class were going out themselves to the cinema or something on Friday night and they asked us along, but Emma declined for both of us, giving me a look full of innuendo.

Wednesday was half-day, and I was going to town to get some new clothes. My mother had promised to give me money for them because none of my old stuff fitted me, and I was going to go to all the shops Emma had told me about. She couldn't come with me herself, but she had given me advice on exactly what stuff in the shops would suit me. When I got there I saw some deadly stuff alright, but I wished Emma had come in with me because when I tried on the clothes she had recommended, some of them were awful, and the rest looked hideous on me. But I managed to pick out some really nice things in a shop I had taken a particular liking to and had gone back to after looking in all the other ones.

God only knows what the name of it was, in fact I don't even know if it had a name. It was upstairs from a record shop on a side street off a side street off a cobbled side street, and it was by reference to the record shop that Emma had told me where it was.

There are mainstream clothes shops that deliberately look ware-housey and rough-and-ready for effect; this was not one of them. This place was a genuine ramshackle dump, with plaster peeling off the brick walls and the carpet so worn in places I nearly tripped over a nail that once held it down and had worked its way loose in time. There was one light bulb dangling from a wire in the roof, but it was so bright and there were so many mirrors you couldn't miss all the fabulous clothes which made you forget on the spot your fears that the roof might cave in on you. No wonder, Emma was telling me, this place made a fortune.

The girl in the shop loved the clothes on me, especially with my hair.

'I'd kill to have hair like that,' she said. Her own she had bleached blonde in the effort, and she thought it looked terrible. It didn't though, it was quite nice, and I told her I liked it.

'You'd know it wasn't natural though,' she sighed.

Anyway, she looked so deadly she didn't need to worry about a little thing like that, and I felt good that she liked the stuff I was buying. She advised me to get my nose pierced like hers to complete the look. I told her I'd be killed, and she rolled her eyes.

'The oul pair, is it? You don't have to tell me. Believe me, I know. What about your ears?'

'One hole in each, only I'm allergic to most earrings.'

'There's some lovely ones over here, and you'd be able to wear them, they're hypo- whatever you call it, they'd look deadly on you.'

She left me at a mirror and returned a few moments later with them. They were nice, two little silver crosses at the end of a short line of black beads, they'd match my choker, but I couldn't afford them. The girl looked at the owner who laughed.

'Give them to her for whatever she has, seeing as she's spending all her money here,' she winked at me, shouting over the Nirvana tape.

'Thanks a million,' I said.

'Not at all, so long as you remember to come back to us in future.'

I put them on and looked in the mirror. I was wearing a long blue-and-black tie-dyed dress, and I held my other stuff up to me.

'I love your make-up,' the girl said, 'it really suits you, with your colouring and your hair.'

I was wearing my usual foundation and a bit of eyeliner. 'How do you think a darker shade would look?' I asked her.

'Awful, leave it the way it is.'

I looked again, and decided that I liked it. I got changed, paid for everything and left. It was getting late anyway so I didn't have the time to go looking at make-up, even if I'd had the money and wanted to, so I went straight home. My mother actually liked the stuff, and said that me and Emma would make a fine pair now and laughed.

The next day, Emma asked eagerly if I'd got anything, and I described everything to her, including the jewellery they'd given to me cheap.

'Did you not like any of the stuff I told you about?'

'Well I did, but they didn't really suit me.'

'Did they not? Oh well, suit yourself.' She was trying to finish off some homework so she didn't say anything else.

On Thursday morning, I didn't see Emma until little break because we were in different subjects up till then. When I found her, she rushed over to me looking excited and dragged me outside, and into a corner where nobody could hear us.

'Me and Brenda have found you the perfect fella. His name's Kev, and he's dead on. He's quiet, but he's one of the nicest blokes I've ever come across. At first we couldn't decide between him and somebody else, but when we saw him last night up the village, I just knew he was the right one for you.'

'Well, I hope you didn't say anything to him. I have to see him and talk to him first,' I said nervously.

'Don't worry, I said nothing to him, well I just said was he going out Saturday night, and he said he was, and I said that was great, I'd see him then. Then I said I had this friend from school coming over to stay with me that night, and she'd be there, and he said "yeah?", and I said "yeah, her name's Cassandra, and she's really nice, I know you'd like her. She's very good looking as well..."' she laughed.

'Oh, Emma, you didn't. I'll kill you.'

'Relax, will you, I didn't say it like that, I just said it real casually, so that he'll remember you when the time comes, so that we won't have to do all the groundwork on the night, and it'll be much less obvious.'

'I don't have a fucking clue what you're on about.'

'Trust me.'

'You wish.'

'Don't worry about it, you don't have to go near him if

you don't want to, but I know you will. You two are going to get along so well together.'

She talked about nothing else all day. I felt wary, in case it didn't work out, but sometimes as excited as she was, in case it did, and she seemed to think it would. I alternated between both emotions, and a lot of the time I felt both at once, but I told myself I wouldn't know what to do until the time came, and I wouldn't have to go ahead until the time came.

Emma constantly reassured me and encouraged me. On Friday in the toilets, she fell around laughing against the door in the middle of telling me some story about him. The door opened outwards, flinging Emma forwards and against the corner of the hand-dryer.

'OW,' she moaned.

'Jesus, are you alright?' It was Natasha standing there, looking horrified until she saw that Emma was not seriously hurt and I was standing beside her. Her face sunk into sulkiness and thinly veiled antipathy.

Emma noticed this too. 'Well I'd be a lot better if some people watched where they were going.'

'It's not my fault, how was I supposed to know you were standing there?'

'I'm sorry, you're dead right, it was my fault,' Emma said sweetly. 'I was just so busy laughing over something this fella did. He's fucking mad, he is, and Cassandra might be going out with him. She's looking for a decent fella, you see, not some fucking sackhead like that Gary bloke.'

Emma picked up her bag and walked out. I followed her, speechless.

'What the fuck did you have to go and say that for?' I

65

demanded angrily as soon as were out of earshot. 'You know bloody well she hates my guts, and she'll just be worse now.'

'No, she won't, and anyway, so what? She's just going on like the spoilt-rotten little bitch she is, now that things aren't going the way she wants them for once, and she deserves everything she gets. And she hurt me, Ow!' Emma touched her forehead with a pained expression, and we had to sit down while she recovered.

She was in slight pain for the rest of the day, and the sight of Natasha or the mention of her name pissed her off so much I didn't bring up the subject again. Instead I asked her some more about Kev.

'Would you go out with him?' I asked.

'No, I wouldn't.'

'Why not?'

'Because he's not my type, but he's perfect for you.'

'How do you know?'

'I just do. I can't explain it, you'll know when you see him yourself.'

And so went Friday.

CHAPTER 7

On Saturday afternoon, I put on the long blue-and-black tie-dyed dress the girl in the shop had liked so much on me and painstakingly applied my make-up. Then I fixed my hair and sprayed it like Emma had showed me. I was getting better at it, though it still took some time.

All day there had been a pain growing in the bottom of my stomach, that's how I get when I'm nervous about something that's about to happen. I'm able to eat, but food is tasteless and has no impact on my hunger or lack of hunger, and so I usually don't bother with it. My hands don't shake, but become quite clumsy, so it takes great concentration and effort to get them to do what I want them to. I bump into things, but don't feel much pain, I feel like I'm numbed after an injection, so things seem to be happening at a far-off distance, and I can't sleep. I didn't sleep much on Friday night, but I wasn't tired, just spaced out.

I checked my bag one last time and packed in my make-up and hair stuff now that I was finished with them. I was dressed in what I was going to wear that night and was not bringing any spare clothes in case Emma would want to borrow them. I felt very mean about it, but after what happened to my waistcoat, I didn't want her wearing any of my clothes again. It made me feel especially bad considering that she'd be more than happy to lend me any of her stuff, but I was not going to change my mind about it. I closed the bag, opened it again to check that I had everything, then closed it, then opened it again to put in my umbrella because it was overcast and it might rain – it'd been raining earlier on – though I hoped it wouldn't, and I was only going to wear my denim jacket. It was quite a mild day, but it might get colder later on; no, it wouldn't, because the forecast had said it would be a mild, warm night, and the jacket was lined, anyway. Stop worrying, Cassandra. I put my jacket on, put my bag on my shoulder and went downstairs.

'I'm off now.'

'Do you not want anything to eat before you go?'

'No, I'm fine, thanks.'

'Are you sure? Okay then, we'll see you sometime tomorrow afternoon. Enjoy yourself.'

'Thanks, bye.'

Soon a bus came and I got on. Looking at the time printed on my bus ticket I saw I was probably going to be way too early. Oh well, it was better than getting off the bus and waiting for the next one which mightn't come.

I sat down on a seat near the window and furtively looked around to see what sort of people were on the bus, but I could only see a few old people, some middle-aged, and women with small screaming kids like you always see downstairs on buses. I glued my eyes to the window, terrified I'd miss my stop, even though Emma had described it thoroughly and assured me I couldn't go wrong because the bus always stopped there for at least five minutes.

The bus passed through Ashford, and the next town and the next town, all relatively familiar red-brick territory, and then out onto the main road, jolting along, stopping and starting at all the bus stops, letting people on, and letting people off, onto a wide dual-carriageway with many exits and entrances to numerous factories and industrial estates; then these faded away and housing estates began to appear along the outskirts of the city, estates with small houses in fading white-wash surrounded by grey concrete walls. We turned off the main road at the sign for Kilmore Village. We drove past a petrol station and down a narrower road between two estates which I didn't pay much attention to because I was too busy straining to see further down the road to where my stop would be. Then we drove past a church, a row of small shops, and a chipper, before stopping in front of a supermarket on the corner with a big enough parking space in front of it.

A crowd was waiting. Most of the people on the bus got off, and I followed them, positive that this was my stop, even though I couldn't see Emma. The place looked about right. I stood at the bus shelter, watching people queue for the bus, which stopped for around ten minutes before moving on. Left alone, I looked at my watch and saw that it was still five minutes before Emma had promised to come to meet me. I wished now I hadn't been so early. I sat down to wait on the low wall separating the path from the car park, and had a look around.

The place was filthy, covered in litter and ashes and discarded cigarette butts, remnants from the bus-waiters.

Directly across the road from me was a sweetshop with a bin outside overflowing with rubbish. Common enough sights anywhere you go, but particularly depressing here in Kilmore Village, where the shops were as shabby and grey as the crumbling wall I was sitting on and the overcast sky above me. I looked behind at the supermarket, newer and in red brick so the graffiti didn't show up so badly, but it was still littered outside from kids hastily tearing up and flinging away the wrappers of their after-shopping treats.

'I told you to put that in the bin,' a mother said to one of them, shushing the baby, taking it out of the trolley seat, and opening the car.

'It's full, Ma,' her five-year-old boy answered her. He was chubby, pasty-faced and bad-tempered, with mousy-brown hair cropped to his head and his clothes hanging out all over the place.

'I don't care, go and pick it up. And would you ever tuck yourself in.'

This he did, with a long and covetous stare at the brightly painted metal horse that you could ride up and down for about two minutes for twenty pence. His mother threw the white plastic bags in the boot of the car.

'Ma, can I've a go on the horsie?'

'No, I told you you could have sweets or a go on the horsie, one or the other and you picked sweets, right?' She finished packing the boot.

'Ah please, Ma.'

'No.'

She stood up. She looked quite young, mid-to-late twenties, very skinny, with her hair dyed blonde; fake-looking, but she had had the roots recently done. She looked exhausted, and the baby was beginning to scream again.

'Ah, go on, Ma.'

'I said no. Would you stop annoying me.' She shoved him into the car, pushed her trolley away, and drove off. God love her, what a little brat.

I stayed where I was. People passed in little groups, women with babies and small children, men, women, no Emma. Often gangs of teenagers passed, right by me, or on the other side of the road, sometimes looking at me curiously, probably wondering who I was, though that was a bit strange, considering in a big place like this, you couldn't know absolutely everyone. Still, Emma had told me that you ended up knowing everyone because everyone around here was sound, and the ones you didn't know, your friends would know them. Or maybe they did know who I was. That was just as bad, seeing as I didn't know who they were. I kept my eyes steadily glued to the ground.

All sorts passed, loads of ravers, and normal people, girls and girls, boys and boys, girls and boys, all sauntering leisurely, going into the newsagent, or walking around the corner to where I assumed the pool hall Emma had told me about and the chipper were. Sometimes girls or boys on their own scurried past, all in a hurry to be someplace else, to meet people, because in places like this, everyone had friends, and thought up things to do, and went out together. Because you had to do something, Emma said; otherwise, you'd be bored out of your fucking mind, because there was nothing else besides the pool hall and a crappy disco once a month in that kip of a community centre that nobody went to. Just as well they were all well able to entertain themselves.

Emma was now twenty minutes late. I wasn't worried as such, seeing as punctuality wasn't exactly one of the good things about her, and she'd told me that the buses were so bad that she didn't expect me to be on time. But I did wish she'd hurry up because the waiting was only making me more nervous.

I was beginning to think I might have got the arrangements wrong and was seriously panicking when I saw Emma from a distance down the road with another girl, obviously Brenda, and I got a good look at her while they were walking towards me. I saw Brenda had all her raver gear on, baggy green jeans and a red wax jacket. She was always on at Emma to dress like that; she thought she'd make a deadly raver, but Emma always told her to fuck off. And then Brenda'd tell her to fuck off herself, she only dressed like she did and listened to metal and sixties' and seventies' rock and stuff because she thought Paul'd fancy her if she did. They had terrible fights from time to time, those two, but it didn't matter because they didn't really mean it and they always made up after. Brenda's mousy brown hair was in a tight corkscrew perm and the front of it was glued up and back into a little bump of a bun. She had thick brown foundation or something on, and bright red lipstick. She wasn't much taller than Emma, but her build made her look much bigger: she was very broad, and she wasn't muscly or chubby, but sort of well-built and stocky. She had a – I don't know what you'd call it – a supercilious look on her face as she looked around her, and I was a bit frightened of her. Now, that's stupid, remember what Emma said about her, remember Emma said that those who don't know her or don't like her think she's real snotty, but she's not, she's a lovely person when you get to know her. She just doesn't take any shit from anyone, that's all.

'Howya,' Emma said, coming up to me. 'Sorry we're a bit late. Are you waiting long?'

'About half an hour,' I said reproachfully.

'Half an hour? Oh you're not serious, I didn't think you'd be here that long. It's all Brenda's fault, she was minding her little brother and sister and we had to wait for her mam to get back before we could go.'

'That's right, blame it all on me, why don't you, you were late knocking up to me, anyway.'

'Not that late, I wasn't. Sorry Cassandra, this is Brenda, as you've probably gathered, and Brenda, this is Cassandra.'

'Hi,' I smiled at her.

'Alright,' she said back to me. 'Emma's told me loads about you. I heard all about the disco last Friday night. Sickener for that Natasha one. She sounds like a right bitch. I feel real sorry for Emma having to go to that school. At least she's got you, though. That's something, anyway.'

'Will we head or what?' Emma asked. 'It's getting late and Mam's desperate to give Cassandra her dinner. There's not much to see around here anyway. It'll keep.'

'I don't mind,' I said, and we started to walk down the road.

'So what do you think of this kip?' Brenda asked.

73

'It's alright,' I said cautiously, smiling at her in a way that I hoped looked friendly and not stupid.

'Do you think?' she laughed disparagingly. 'It's alright I suppose, nothing like where you're from, of course. Still, though, they're all mad snobby over there. You can't have everything, I suppose.'

'Cassandra can walk into town, she doesn't have to get the bus.'

'Yeah? That'd be deadly, the money you'd save on bus fares. I'd love to live near town. Do you go in much?'

'Once in a while, I do.'

'Is that all? I'd go in all the time, I would. But I suppose I'd get sick of it, alright, if I actually lived there.'

'This is it now,' Emma announced.

It was an estate of small semi-detached houses, which were built in a sort of concrete and mostly painted white. Some looked better kept than others. Each had a driveway the width of a car up to the front door and a small lawn beside it. Some lawns had bushes and flower-beds and trees along them, some had none, and some people had extended the concrete driveway right across to the dividing wall, making the place look worse. God knows, there was enough drab concrete around, though it was practical, seeing as the rain turns grass to slushy wet muck and there were a lot of kids around. There were shiny new cars parked at some of the doors, rusting old bangers, or vans, or nothing, outside others. The place seemed to be crawling with kids and the noise level was sky high; the sound of playing and messing and fighting.

'It is my imagination, or are there more kids out than usual?' Emma asked Brenda, who shrugged.

'Don't know, there was no-one out all morning because it was pissing rain, and it was raining all yesterday as well, so they're probably all coming out now. Downer or what.'

I didn't mind, though.

'It's not as bad as having to listen to heavy traffic all the time,' I said.

They looked at me as if I was completely off my head.

'Whatever you're into,' Brenda said.

We passed a house that was blaring out rave. 'For fuck sake,' Emma said. 'That's Dave's gaff, you'll probably see him later. He's friends with Kev.'

Emma and Brenda looked at each other slyly and knowingly.

'Kev's going to be there tonight,' Brenda said to me. 'So things seem to be going to plan.'

'Let's just play things by ear.' I smiled tentatively.

Brenda shrugged. 'Whatever. It's all up to you, anyway.' She paused at an open gateway. 'This is my gaff, by the way. I have to go in now, so I'll see youse later.'

Emma led me to another house across the road and a few doors down, a house recently painted and well kept with flower-beds in the front garden, though there were few flowers left, this time of year.

'And now you finally get to see where I live,' Emma said disparagingly.

She opened the front door and I followed her into a narrow hallway with a staircase about a half a yard from the door, all carpeted in thickly piled bright red, with white-and-red-striped wallpaper.

'Mam, we're back,' she called, flinging her jacket on the small hallstand that took up all the space between the stairs and the front door, and indicating for me to do the same and leave my bag there. I followed her into the surprisingly large kitchen (it was actually an extension, which took up a lot of the tiny back garden), where there was a woman, in blue jeans and a green jumper, tall, thin, with a lined face and no make-up. But her shoulder-length hair was impeccably styled and dyed blacker than black, like Emma's, only coarser and stringier.

'Hello Cassandra, I'm Emma's mam. You're very welcome here,' she smiled, shaking my hand.

'Thanks a lot.'

'Sit down there, I have your dinner ready for you. Do you like chicken and potatoes?'

'Yes please.'

'That's great.'

She put my dinner in front of me, then Emma's, then her own.

'Help yourself there to anything you want, take some Coke. Emma's dad's not here. He said to tell you he'd see you later.'

The talk went on like this for the rest of the meal and dessert, while Emma said nothing. I was surprised that her mother seemed to be so nice, because Emma had made her out to be horrible.

'We're going upstairs now, Mam,' Emma announced, standing up. 'And we'll be going out fairly soon.'

'Oh yes, another night out and about God only knows where and with who until all hours,' she said. 'Just be good, Emma and stay out of trouble.'

'Yeah, right Mam.'

'Don't you right Mam me. I worry about you. I bet

Cassandra here doesn't have to make deals with her parents about studying in school. Did she tell you about that? How I've to let her have one night a week when she can stay out till twelve wherever she wants if I expect her to study?'

Emma smiled at me knowingly from behind her mother's back.

'Yes she did,' I said awkwardly.

'Well I don't like it, especially not at that hour, when there's all drunks coming out of the pubs. Still, as long as she's with people, and there's no drinking or messing, I'll keep my side of the bargain.' She looked at Emma warningly.

Emma kept an innocent face on while we left the kitchen. I went into the small toilet next door.

When I came out, Emma was waiting, and I followed her upstairs with my bag and into her room.

She shut the door behind me, and leaned against it with an air of great relief. 'Thank God that's over, anyway.'

'But she's really nice.'

'She's alright, I suppose, until she starts on about "and where are you off to tonight?" Anyway, she was licking the arse off you, being all nice and that, because you're a "suitable friend", a "nice well-mannered girl from that lovely school".'

'Did she say that about me?'

'Yeah, just there now, when I was talking to her on my own in the kitchen.'

The doorbell rang.

'That'll be Brenda, wait there a second.'

I looked around, listening for the sound of the door opening and voices. Emma's room was actually two rooms

77

knocked into one, across the landing from her parents' and the bathroom. That was about it upstairs. There was just the kitchen/dining room, the sitting room, and a toilet downstairs. In here there was a single bed and a folded camp bed with bedclothes in the corner, obviously for me – to have set it up in advance meant taking up the greater amount of space in the room. There was a desk with shelves above it containing Emma's school books, some more shelves with hi-fi and tapes, no books, a wardrobe, no dressing table, a mirror balanced on the narrow window sill, hairbrush, lotion and moisturiser on one side of it, and an open make-up bag and scattered make-up on the other. Cans of mousse and hairspray were thrown on the pink flowery carpet. The white wallpaper was sprigged with matching pink flowers, but most of it was hidden by the posters she'd told me about.

'I see you tidied your room,' Brenda said, walking in, wearing the same clothes as earlier.

'Yeah, I had to, my mam kept bitching me about it. "Now Emma, you can't invite a guest over to sleep in a messy room." You wouldn't mind, would you?' she asked me.

'No,' I said.

Emma tied her hair up and smeared cream all over her face. She walked over to the wardrobe and pulled out some clothes. 'I'm just going to the bathroom to get changed. You two start getting ready.'

She went out, taking her make up and hair stuff with her, leaving me alone in the room with Brenda.

Brenda unpacked a small bag, cleaned off her old make-up and started applying moisturiser in Emma's mirror. I did the same, using the mirror in my compact.

'Looking forward to tonight?' Brenda asked from the window.

'Yeah.'

'Me, too.'

'Will the fella you're meeting be there?'

'No. He's going with someone else as of yesterday.'

'I'm sorry about that.'

'Don't be. Little pricks like that are no good for anything more than getting your bit, and I was getting bored with him anyway.'

'I see,' I said.

Emma returned, dressed, hair and face done. She was wearing a long green crushed velvet top that buttoned from about half-way up, her black stretch jeans and suede boots, and about three gold crosses around her neck.

'What do youse think?'

'You look deadly,' I answered, and Brenda, turning her head from the mirror, agreed.

'Hurry up there, you. We don't have all night, you know,' she said to Brenda. 'Give us a look,' she said to me and I turned to face her.

'Did you not get a darker shade of make-up,' she asked.

'No, like I didn't have any money left after buying my clothes, and I like this colour, anyway.'

'Well, whatever you think yourself. If I were you, though, I'd at least take off the eyeliner. It's bad enough having your eyes bulging out of your face without making them worse.'

Both of them burst out laughing.

'Bulging out of her face? That is bad, Emma.'

'She knows I'm only messing with her. Anyway, I don't mean it like that. Besides, friends have to tell each other the truth about these things, don't they, Cassandra?'

I was struggling not to let on how much her words stung. My parents had always told me that my eyes were beautiful, but often, when I was a kid, I'd been called a zombie because of them, and I'd always been sensitive about them since.

'Yes, that's true,' I said calmly. 'But I read in a magazine that on eyes like mine, it's better to put a little bit of make-up than none at all, because otherwise they look too bare,' I improvised.

'Well, they're your eyes,' Emma said, insinuating that she still thought they'd look better her way, and so to please her, I rubbed some of the eyeliner away.

Brenda turned around. 'Ready now,' she announced, and put on her jacket.

I hastily took out my brush and hairspray and touched my hair up in front of the mirror. 'Ready,' I said.

'You look nice,' Brenda said.

Emma handed me a pendant on a long silver chain. 'Put this on and see how it looks.'

I put it on with misgivings.

'That's perfect, do you want to wear it?' she asked.

'I'd love to, but I can't. If I wear this, I'll get a rash.'

'Pity, it's deadly on you,' Brenda said.

'Do you think?' I asked, looking at it again. It wasn't particularly nice, but I was staying in Emma's house and going out with all her friends so I didn't want to hurt their feelings.

'Ah, go on, wear it,' Emma encouraged, looking at me beseechingly. 'Those magazines you were talking about always say you have to suffer to be beautiful.'

'Alright then, I'll wear it,' I said, and both of them smiled delightedly.

We went downstairs and me and Emma put on our jackets, her preening proudly in the little mirror as she carefully adjusted her beloved biker. Then we said goodbye to Emma's mam, who again warned her to be good. Emma slung her empty schoolbag onto her back (to stash the drink in, she said) and the three of us left the house.

CHAPTER 8

It was dark now, and cool, but at least it was dry, and the ground had dried up since the morning's rain. We hurried down towards the village because the two of them were dying for a smoke, and didn't dare light up until they were safe within the confines of the pool hall or with a group outside the chipper, or up the convenient lane next to the chipper.

The village looked better now that it was dark, and the lights were on. And it was busier. Outside the chipper a crowd had already gathered, mainly ravery, some normal, and two weird looking fellas with long hair. One was hastily introduced to me by a girl called Aoife as her boyfriend Brian before I was swept away from him up the lane with Emma and Brenda so that they could have their smokes. Emma whispered to me that her and Brian hated each other from way back after she split up with a member of his band. The other fella was Mick, Paul's brother, another member of the band. He hated her as well. But they were fucking weirdos anyway. You wouldn't mind them.

She kicked a beer can that was standing against a skip and it spilled out all over the dirty grey ground. 'Pity that can was opened or we could have drunk it,' Emma said.

Brenda gave her a disgusted look. 'Scummy bitch. That stuff's like dog's piss.'

It looked just like dog piss as well, that sickly colour running and streaking and soaking into the ground in patches, and I felt revolted.

A few more girls came up the lane. These were welcomed enthusiastically and I was introduced as 'My friend Cassandra from school'. One was the famous Michelle, definitely a raver, and fairly good-looking, with blonde curly hair. Emma was jumping all over her with welcome. I thought she didn't like Michelle at the moment, oh well, they must have made up.

Michelle smiled at me. 'You in that school as well? Oh jaysus, you poor thing,' before commencing a heated conversation with the others about who was buying their drink.

Emma said smugly that she had arrangements made for me, her and Brenda with someone who wouldn't get into the offo for any more people. Michelle said she had some spare blow, and Emma negotiated to maybe buy some of it, because she hadn't had a chance to get some herself earlier on. Then we all left the lane, the others to persuade someone to buy their drink, and Emma to find the girl that had promised to get ours.

At the chipper, Emma introduced me to the new-comers. I relaxed, sitting beside Brenda and another girl on the worn-away beige-and-brown-tiled window sill, lean-ing against the wide glass front, but not too hard, in case I fell through. Emma spotted an older girl down the road and ran to her with our money. Things were slowly being organised. The older-looking ones were buying drink for as many as they could manage. Those who were left short grabbed and begged older brothers and sisters, neighbours, acquaintances, anyone who was or looked eighteen until finally everyone was taken care of.

Emma returned with a bulging schoolbag and casually walked up the lane where she emptied half the cans into Brenda's bag, concealing them under a shirt. Brenda then slung her bag onto her back equally casually. People started leaving then, in groups of twos or threes so that no passer-by would guess there was a gang of us making our way to the night's designated drinking spot. Everyone was excited and friendly and I began to feel at home and to enjoy myself. The atmosphere was great, high spirits, secrecy and complicity. It was going to be a good night.

When we got there, the drink was distributed. Emma opened her bag, took out a can for her and one for me, stuck another one in her jacket and told me to watch nothing happened to the bag because our drink was in it. She cracked open her can and knocked it against Brenda's. They said 'down the hatch' in unison and took a long slug each.

I opened mine and took a few tentative sips. It tasted much nicer than I remembered, out here in the cool night air. We sat there together against the high, grey wall for a few minutes, sitting on plastic bags so that our arses wouldn't get dirty, even though the muck was hard and dry and we probably wouldn't have gotten more than a bit dusty. There was only about twelve here. I'd got the impression there was going to be a bigger crowd.

'Is this all that's coming?'

'No, there'll be more coming later,' Emma said and Brenda laughed. 'Getting anxious for your fella, are you?'

I had been trying to get that out of my head. Michelle and her friends arrived and Emma and Brenda rushed over to talk to them, muttering something along the lines of 'back in a minute, mind the drink'. I waited on my own for about ten minutes, furtively glancing over at them where they sat. I was probably meant to mix with the others, but they were all engrossed in dramas of their own, so I sat there, drinking my can of Fosters. My head was beginning to buzz, and thankfully I was beginning to relax, and loosen up.

'You're Emma's friend, aren't you?'

I looked up and smiled, trying to place her in my head. Not a raver: blue jeans, black jacket, shoulder-length black hair; who the fuck was she again?

'Yeah, Cassandra.'

'Cassandra, that's what it is. I'm Jane, I saw you over here on your own, and I thought you might want to come over to us.'

She pointed to Mick and Brian, sitting at a distance from everyone else. Emma didn't like them, but she'd never mentioned this girl Jane, and she seemed really nice.

'Sure, I'm meant to be waiting for Emma, but . . .'

'She'll come looking for you when she wants you, she's tied up for the moment, anyway.'

I gathered up all the stuff and followed Jane.

'This is Cassandra, lads. Cassandra, Mick my fella, and Brian.'

'Howya.'

'Alright.'

I smiled, greeted them, sat down and drank some more.

'We don't usually drink with this gang,' Jane continued. 'But Brian's going with Aoife and he didn't want to come here on his own, so we came along too.'

'Well do you blame me?' Brian asked. 'I mean, fucking Emma and Brenda are here. Headwrecking or what.'

'Shut up, will you, Cassandra's a friend of Emma's from school,' Jane said.

'Yeah? What's a nice girl like you doing with a bitch like that?' Mick asked, shaking back his long, blond hair. It was fabulous, right down his back. Like Brian's, only Brian's was more browny.

I opened my second can. My head was spinning and I felt great. I was on a high, and all my nerves, anxieties, fears and hang-ups had disappeared.

'I like her, she's my friend.'

'Until something better comes along. She's a two-faced, using bitch,' Brian said.

'Let's just drop the subject and enjoy the night,' Jane urged.

'Fine by me, I've got better things to do than sit around talking about Emma. Just don't say we didn't warn you,' Mick said to me, knocking back a large portion of his can in one slurp.

'Emma told me youse hated her,' I said.

'Yeah, and did she tell you why?' Brian asked.

'No.'

'Bet she didn't. I'll tell you what happened. You see, we're in this band, right, me, Mick and a few of the lads, and one of them, Tomo, was mad into Emma for yonks, and she wouldn't go near him. Then, finally, at the

86

beginning of the summer, she said yes, she'd go with him, and he was delighted. But she'd never, like, get off with him or anything. She'd make all sorts of stupid excuses, and she'd only ever go anywhere with him if he was knocking up to Mick's on the way,' Brian said significantly.

Jane saw that I didn't understand, so she explained. 'You see, all the girls around, especially our age, are mad into Mick's brother, Paul, who's eighteen. They follow him around the place and everything. And they think they have a chance and all, because his friend, Johno, told the world about the fourteen-year-old girlfriend he had on holiday in England last year.'

'They don't have a hope though. My brother's the biggest bastard around, but he got enough slagging over cradle-snatching last time around to do it again in a hurry. He's too busy shagging girls his own age anyway.'

'Shut up, would you, and let me get on with it,' Brian said. 'Emma kept on knocking up to Mick's with Tomo and asking casually if Paul was around. Only Paul's never around. So then she'd make an excuse and say she had to go off home, and this happened so often, we got suspicious, and said it to Tomo, only he wouldn't believe a word of it. He was mad into her, you see. Then about two weeks later we all went drinking, and Emma and Brenda came along. Tomo was going to be late. Someone had brought along this fella, Anto, who wasn't from around here. Anyway, when Tomo arrived, he was in bits, because on his way up, he had found Emma, locked out of her head and all over Anto.'

'She probably didn't mean it,' I defended.

They shrugged, and started talking about music. In spite of what they'd said about Emma, they were all sound, especially Jane, and we talked away, while I finished my second can and made heavy inroads into my third and final can.

'There you are. I've been looking everywhere for you,' Emma said, pulling me to my feet. 'Are you having a good time?' she asked, falling on me in a big hug while I struggled to take the weight of her, being unsteady on my own feet. I failed, and we both fell to the ground, Jane grabbing my can before it spilt. Emma laughed drunkenly and laid her head on my shoulder. Her breath stank of drink and smoke.

'I'm fucking stoned out of my head I am,' she murmured. 'I've just had half Michelle's ten-spot as well as two cans. Where's me other can? Giveus it!'

'Don't let her drink any more,' Jane whispered firmly.

Emma lifted her head and gave the other three a filthy look. 'Don't youse tell me what to do. I bet you've been telling my friend all sorts of bullshit about me.'

She lunged forth as if to hit them, but I pulled her back. She laughed and hugged me again. 'Let's go sit with Brenda, I don't like it here.'

I said goodbye apologetically to the others, while Emma gave them more vicious looks. We found Brenda, leaning against a tree, as stoned and out of it as Emma, and they decided to save their remaining drink for another time.

Brenda suddenly disappeared to talk to some people, while Emma whispered to me not to listen to what Mick and Brian said about her.

'I only went with Tomo out of pity, and I regretted it as

soon as I said yes, only I didn't know how to break it to him, and I didn't mean to go off with Anto, only I couldn't help myself, I was locked, and he was a fucking ride. You believe me, don't you?'

She looked at me anxiously and I said, 'Of course I believe you, I'm your friend, amn't I?' and she hugged me.

'You are so sound,' she said, and I was so happy.

Brenda rushed back, full of glee.

'Kev wants to meet you. He thinks you're gorgeous.'

Emma and Brenda shrieked with joy and I begged them to for fuck sake shut up, embarrassment and fear back despite the drink, which must have been wearing off. They pointed him out to me. Not dead ugly, but a bit ugly, and he looked like an imbecile, short hair, slithering like slimy grease with gel that slinked it back behind sticky-out ears.

'He's worse than Gary,' I said.

'Don't be so mean,' Emma remonstrated. 'Looks aren't everything, and he's dead on.'

'Still, though.'

'Beggars can't be choosers,' Brenda said meaningfully.

'And he's harmless,' Emma encouraged. 'He's not like the other dirty bastards around here, he won't lay a finger on you except to get off with you.'

'I don't know, Emma. No, I don't want to.' I looked at them beseechingly, struggling to escape the force of their eyes willing me to say yes.

'You can't say no, it'd break his heart,' Emma said with an air of finality and impatience.

I looked at her, confused now. Only a minute ago she'd been saying it had been wrong of her to go with Tomo out of pity and all week she'd said I didn't have to do it if I didn't want to. It must have been the drink, but she was looking at me strangely with a glacial gaze that I didn't understand. It was almost as though she hated me, even though I said don't be stupid, Cassandra, you're as pissed as she is. But my heart was twisting with pain, and I was so locked I felt like a little kid and I wanted nothing more than to please her, to make the look go away. My throat went dry and constricted, and I felt a bursting cramp across my stomach and realised I must have been dying to go to the toilet for at least half an hour.

'Alright, but I'm dying to have a piss.'

Emma gave me a look of pride. 'Brenda'll go and tell him, and I'll show you where to piss.'

She led me to a distant spot behind a hedge and kept sketch while I fertilised the earth in floods. At least I felt better after that, but I was sobering up, so I gulped the third or so that was left of my can, quickly, to top up my buzz and numb my nerves. I could drink it like it was water now.

Giggling, Brenda led me to another secluded spot where Kev was waiting alone, posing against an evergreen tree like an arrogant bastard. She introduced us, telling me to sit down there, while she stood making small talk until she said she had to go, giving us sly looks as she went, me looking after her helplessly.

There was an awkward silence. He took a swig of his can. I looked at it covetously, longing to silence my screaming nerves.

'D'you want some?'

'Eh, yeah.'

I took the can and took a long desperate slug. I took so much in one go, that I swallowed back, almost choking, but I managed not to cough out loud. When I felt calmer, I handed back the can. My fingers brushed against his, which felt cold, pasty, and greasy. I stiffened, and he must have taken that as encouragement because he took my hand, put the can down, moved closer, and put his sticky lips on mine. His breath tasted like the smell of a pan that has been left forgotten in the cooker for weeks, and when you open the cooker and take it out, the air is fouled, and you stand there staring in revulsion at a big mess of solidified grease mixed in with bits of rotting chicken or whatever meat that was cooked and eaten at some long-forgotten meal.

I bore this for a few minutes. He tried to stick his tongue in my mouth, but I resisted, and feeling guilty, bore his embrace for another little while before he broke away for air and I took the opportunity to move away, look at my watch and say, 'Oh God, it's getting late, I have to find Emma and go to the toilet,' feeling that I'd done my duty.

'Fair enough. See you again, then.'

'What? Oh, yeah, bye.'

I walked out of sight and leaned against a tree in relief, trying to swallow back the taste of scum in my mouth. Never again, I promised myself, nursing the small consolation that it was a huge load off my mind to have finally been with someone. Like all the other girls. But that had been horrible, and the revulsion loomed large in my mind and memory, replaying over and over and over again in all its original intensity. I couldn't get it out of my head. It just wouldn't go away.

I walked towards the main body of the group.

Michelle saw me and ran towards me. 'They told me you were off meeting Kev, how did you get on?' She looked at my face and gave me a big hug of sympathy. 'Don't tell me, I know, I was with him before. He tastes disgusting. If only I'd known beforehand, I'd have told you not to go anywhere near him.'

Emma and Brenda saw us, and rushed towards us, full of excitement and anticipation. They slowed down when they got near us, and their faces changed.

'That bad?' Emma asked anxiously.

I wanted to hit her, and that shocked me so much, I felt tears coming out of my eyes instead.

'What's wrong?' Emma seemed surprised and concerned, and Michelle looked at her in disbelief.

'What d'you think's wrong with her, sending her off to shift Kev the Scumbag? And don't say youse didn't know, because I made bloody sure the whole world knew, the girls anyway, after I was with him. Remember?'

'You were never with him,' Brenda insisted.

'Yes I was.'

'Well, you never told us about it.'

'I did.'

'You didn't.'

'Well it was years ago, maybe I didn't.'

She wasn't sure anymore, but continued to insist that they couldn't possibly not have heard about him from the other girls that had had the misfortune to be with him since, while Emma and Brenda continued to deny it.

'Come over here, Cassandra.' Emma assumed command and led me off on my own to talk while I wiped away silent tears, thoroughly ashamed and embarrassed by them.

'So it was awful, was it, I had no idea it'd turn out like this.'

'It's not your fault,' I said, trying to look okay so that Emma wouldn't think I was some sap who started bawling crying at the drop of a hat.

It worked, because Emma's face lightened and cleared up. 'Thank God you're taking it so well, I was afraid you'd be blaming it all on me.'

'Of course not.'

She smiled and gave me a long hug, which comforted me, and I wondered again at the physical affection these girls gave one another, especially when they were drunk.

'You are one of the nicest people I have ever met,' she said. 'I hate that school but I feel a lot better now, going in in the morning, knowing that you'll be there too.'

'Me too.'

I scratched my neck; looking down, I saw a rash, spreading outwards from where Emma's necklace had touched my skin.

She gasped with horror. 'Quick, take it off.'

I gave it to her, and held my hands tightly, resisting the urge to scratch again, knowing how much worse that would make it.

Emma produced a packet of extra-strong mints from her pocket and broke it in two, giving half the packet to me. 'Eat that, so my mam won't get the smell of drink off you.'

We sat there a little while. Michelle and Brenda came

over clutching all their bags. 'Are you alright now?' they asked.

'Yeah, I'm fine.'

'Good. He's gone home now, anyway, so you don't have to worry about running into him,' Michelle said soothingly.

Emma took her deodorant out and passed it round, everyone spraying themselves thoroughly. Then we took turns sniffing each other until we were satisfied that no-one smelt of drink, or any illegal substance. We were all reasonably sober now, so we were fairly confident we wouldn't get snared.

Michelle left to walk home with her friends from her estate and me, Emma and Brenda set off in our own direction. They were being particularly nice to me, and it poured balm on my wounds. But otherwise, I was happy, out here, in this friendly place, with my friend Emma and her friend, Brenda.

We left Brenda at her house and went on to Emma's. No-one was snared, and Emma's mam had bread rolls and buns out for our supper, and Emma was chatty and nice to her mam this time round.

Afterwards, when we went upstairs to bed, Emma continued to talk soothingly about anything and everything but Kev. She was talking about some film she'd seen on the telly last week when she dropped off to sleep.

But I couldn't sleep for a long time, lying there in the narrow camp bed, afraid to move in case the whole thing collapsed and brought the room down around me. Staring at the light shining in from the landing through the keyhole and the bottom of the door. Feeling my nose and ears chill and ache, caught in the draught blowing in from the window. Finally, exhausted, I fell into fits of short unrestful sleep from which I'd wake suddenly in terror, unable to remember what I'd dreamt of. The pattern repeated itself again and again until morning came, and I rose like the living dead, aware of nothing but overwhelming tiredness and a dim consciousness somewhere in the distance.

That was how I had breakfast, got dressed, washed my face and teeth, said goodbye to Emma's mam, was introduced to her da, thanked him, walked to the bus stop with Emma, and waited in the lashing rain, which I barely felt, my umbrella buried, long since forgotten at the bottom of my bag. On the bus, I leaned against the window, and watched Kilmore whirl away, its outlines blurred in a vision of speed and rain-washed glass, listening to the hum of the engine and the beat of the rain.

CHAPTER 9

I got home, did some homework, and talked to my parents without thinking about anything. I was much too busy commanding my brain not to think about last night.

This was more difficult than it used to be, but then I was two years out of practice. I'd had it honed to a fine art in primary school, put everything out of my head as soon as I was out in the evening playing with all my friends – all the kids from our road, playing chasing and hopscotch and Simon Says, out on the middle of the road because the paths were too narrow and the gardens practically non-existent; raging everytime a car drove up and we had to break off the game to stand aside on the path and let the car pass.

Books were good. Especially when they were about nothing I'd ever known. Lose myself in them completely without any unhappy reminders. I never could understand stories about characters who sprung from the pages to join the reader in her or his real life. The point was to forget about real life. Nor stories where the reader jumped into the book and another world. Better to pretend that they might actually like you, so leave yourself out of it, Cassandra. Books saved many lunchtimes too, the perfect excuse for solitude, sitting cramped in the same position for twenty minutes every day, even in winter, in the grey concrete schoolyard. There was a high wall with a gate in the middle and benches all along it. I used to sit there, facing the yard and the main building, grey brick with two classrooms, with all the snot-green prefabs around it, one prefab per class. They were supposed to be building us a bigger school and dumping the prefabs, but they didn't. They'd been saying they would for about twenty years, but they never did. And all the prefabs were falling apart, roofs leaking, windows leaking, walls pulling apart from each other.

I had to sit within view of the staffroom prefab to keep my books from puddles and football and volleyball. That meant more embarrassment, adults seeing me on my own like that.

And all this never went away, it was always lying in my head, and jumping up to torment me whenever I was upset or happy. But the last thing I would do was 'talk it out with someone' or 'get help'. Jesus Christ, that'd be ten times worse. Nothing made me angrier than reading books where the nice teacher or parent made everything alright. Or leaflets on the library counter saying, if this happens to you, tell someone.

Once in a while, maybe once a year, it'd come up in religion. 'Now if you were being bullied or you knew someone who was being bullied, you'd tell a responsible adult, wouldn't you?' the teacher of the time would say, looking at everyone seriously.

'Yes, Miss,' or 'Yes, Sir,' they'd all chant back solemnly in unison, and I'd wish I had the guts to throw my bag at them all and walk out and never ever have to see anyone ever again, but I never did, because this wasn't a book.

Anyway, I wasn't even sure I was being bullied. I wasn't beaten up or hit by anyone like the characters in the leaflets. If I was sitting at the back of the room, I'd be kicked under the table and pinched, but I would fix my legs so they couldn't get them, and position my arms so that it'd be obvious to the teacher and say 'Ow!' as loud as I dared. But the teacher would just say stop the messing back there, so I used to make sure I sat at the top of the room where nobody dared do it.

Nobody stopped me and told me to hand over my pocket money. I just knew nobody liked me. When I had started with the books, I'd been asked to show them what I was reading. I'd hand over the book, have it kicked and thrown and dropped into puddles, pages wet and clinging to each other, the print distorted. But after a while, the books plan worked so well that I felt I didn't deserve the added bonus of loving the books I read and lived for the moment when I was free to pick up at the page where I'd last left off.

God only knows what was wrong with me. I just tried not to think about it. Like now, lying in my bed, at three in the morning with the memory of Kev, allowing myself a crying fit, knowing that if I cried now, it'd be easier to subdue tears later.

One memory in particular hits me harder and deeper than all the others together and follows me in and out of short fits of turbulent sleep.

It was a bright spring day, I was eight, and all the girls had taken to skipping, one at a time, two swinging the long orange rope while all the others waited, impatient. My eyes were drawn from the page by the singing of the rhymes, the rhythm of the feet, and the sound of laughter, of dissension over who was next, and I would have waited patiently and joyously till the end of the earth for just one little go.

One day, outside the classroom, when I was pretending to look for something in the pocket of my coat so I wouldn't have to go out to play just yet, I heard the teacher talking inside the room to the two girls who decided all the games the others would play.

'Cassandra is a very nice girl. Why doesn't she play skipping like everyone else?'

'I don't know.'

'I don't know either.'

'Did you ever ask her?'

'No.'

'Well, I think you should. I think she'd love to skip with you all.'

I rushed to the yard so they wouldn't know I'd heard them, and I was so happy. I could skip, I skipped every night at home with the kids there. I sat down with my book. They came outside and walked towards me. As soon as I saw them, my heart started thumping. What if I missed the rope and ruined the game, they would hate me so much. I could barely speak by the time they reached me, and barely managed to mutter, yeah, okay.

I joined the end of the line, sung the rhyme in my head and gave all my attention to the rhythm of the rope, so I wouldn't miss it. But when my turn came, I jumped in one turn of the rope too late, got the first jump, missed the next, got tangled in the rope, which stopped the game and meant I had to turn the rope, only I turned too fast, and when I was given out to, too slowly, so that I had to give it to somebody else. I stood to the side indecisively and the two in charge came over to me, told me it'd be better if I didn't skip because it ruined it for everyone else, and I said yeah, okay, and went back to my book, my eyes swimming before the page until my senses dulled, like I could make them then, so I was still upset but at least not a cry-baby.

And I knew why this one hit me bad now. It was like with Emma; I'd been offered Emma, a friend like I'd wished for, only I was so afraid of fucking up, I'd probably fuck up anyway. I'd already made a fuck-up of Kev, and the smoke the Friday before, I couldn't afford any more. I'd have to handle myself better. Because I couldn't bear the thought of losing her. Not her. Anyway things were different now. The only reason I had no other friends now was because they were all fucking eejits around here and in school. And I knew that if I knew nothing else.

I'd never been able to figure out why they didn't like me in primary school, but I spent a lot of time listening to their conversations and studying their actions, and their clothes, and their schoolbags and the lunches they brought to school, so that I could make myself the same as them. Then they might like me. It never worked. But at least I learnt enough to know, when we were going to move here, that it was real posh, and only snobs lived there. Fucking eejits and snobs, that was what they'd heard from anyone they knew that'd ever met anyone from around here. So I consoled myself and Aisling with that when we failed to make friends and brushed off as stupid any comments about us being too shy to mix with everyone else.

I felt sick when the time came to get up for school, but I wanted to see Emma, that would make me feel better, especially if she was still in a nice mood. She was, and I felt much better, things would be better now. Emma was still here, wasn't she? And, the most wonderful thing, her friends had all liked me, said to tell me they were asking for me, wanted to know when I was coming out again. They were going out on Friday night – Saturday was too risky, they'd heard some people they knew had been caught by the pigs Saturday night, there were no pigs last Friday. Would I come out again? Her mam loved me, said I could stay over whenever I liked. Kev wouldn't be there, she'd been talking to him and told him I wouldn't be coming out again soon, and he was very disappointed, said this weekend'd be good apart from Friday, he was working, but Emma said no, I wasn't coming out at all, so I had nothing to worry about. Yes, I'd love to come, that'd be deadly, would Jane and Mick and Brian be there too? She looked at me coldly, and I hastened to explain that though she didn't like them because they didn't like her because they'd the wrong idea about her, I liked them. Whatever you're into, she said. No, they won't be there, because they don't actually hang around with us, but everyone else will, Brenda and Michelle, you like them don't you? Yes, I do, and I'd love to come, that'd be deadly. And I was allowed go, once I'd dispelled my parents' concern about was it really alright with her mother, she'd had me over only last Saturday, and so everything would be fine, and the lure of Friday calmed the turbulence that continued to swirl and storm in my head.

CHAPTER 10

It was a quarter-past five by the time the Kilmore bus pulled in across from the supermarket. The place looked much better today, because the rain had cleared up over the last few days, and the sky was crisp and blue. Blustery squalls of wind had set in yesterday and had blown into powerful gusts overnight, so the litter tossed up and down and along the ground.

Brenda met us at the bus stop, already changed out of her school uniform. 'Youse have to hurry up, we're all meeting up in the village an hour early.'

'That means a quarter to seven! Why?' Emma was raging.

'We just are, we want to get out early so the pigs don't catch us, now come on.'

We walked quickly out of the village, down a wildly graffitoed alley so that Emma could have a quick smoke as she walked, then into their estate, Emma cursing as she looked at her watch.

'When will the dinner be ready, Mam?'

'About half-six, love.'

The kitchen clock read twenty to six.

'Half-six! We'll be late, we have to be out of here by then at the latest or they won't wait for us.'

'Who won't wait for youse?'

'The ones we're going out with.'

'I'm sure they will, anyway it's not my fault; you told me last night you'd be leaving at half-seven at the earliest.'

'Well, I thought we were, but we're not now.'

Emma's mam rolled her eyes upwards and hit her with the tea towel in her hand. 'Well I'll do my best for you, right?'

We rushed upstairs, and got changed, and I put on my make-up as fast as I could. Emma's took longer than mine because she had to take off the make-up she'd had on all day in school and put on new stuff. My hair didn't take long, but Emma's did, so she told me to go down and see was the dinner ready when I was done.

Her mam was leaning against the cooker with a paper in her hand.

'Hi,' I said timidly. 'Emma was wondering how the dinner was getting on.'

'I bet she was. It'll be just a minute now. Sit down there. What's she doing? Her hair or her face?'

'Both.'

'I thought as much. She pays too much attention to her looks and messing around up the village. I just hope this new school'll settle her down a bit. How's she getting on there?'

'Fine.'

'Good. I know she didn't want to go, but it's for the best, she had too many distractions up in the other place, and she wasn't doing a tap of work. It's still a hassle getting her down to some study, but at least I haven't had any complaints back about her yet.'

'She's very good at school.' This conversation was embarrassing me. She went to check the dinner, spaghetti bolognese.

'That's great to hear. She still comes in here of an evening, saying she hates the place, but we want her to get a good education. Every time I pick up a paper, there's something in it about unemployment, and how can I expect her to get a job if she won't even study for her Junior Cert, never mind get into college?'

I didn't know what to say to her, to say it was better to be like Emma than boring like the others who wore themselves out studying?

'At least she's got a friend anyway,' she said smiling at me. 'That's something.'

She put the spaghetti out on white plates with pink flowers on them and called Emma. The two of us sat down to eat.

'She's a great one to talk, the dinner's on the table for her and she's still up there fixing her hair.'

Emma rushed in a few minutes later and shovelled down her dinner.

'Mind you don't choke to death,' her mother warned her.

It was twenty to seven. The doorbell rang.

'Go and let Brenda in, will you?' Emma muttered through her food.

Brenda was impatient. 'Are youse ready?'

'Nearly.'

She walked into the kitchen. 'Come on, Emma, we're late.'

Emma shovelled down the last of her food, knocked

back her drink, rushed to the toilet, and finally we were out of there.

We ran all the way up to the village. The light was dimming a bit and the street lights were lighting up. The place was deserted so we had to go and make enquiries in Johnny's, the famous pool hall. I was finally inside it. Wow. Half the under-age population of Kilmore hung around here; the half that mattered.

They weren't here right now though. Just two fellas playing pool at one of the two worn-away pool tables, flicking ash into a plastic ashtray that had cigarette burns right through it. There was another fella lost in a game on one of the machines. There were about four machines, called things like Super Warrior and Champion Boxer and stuff. Then there were two girls sitting smoking in a corner. They were all ravers.

Emma and Brenda went over to the girls, lighting up first, and I followed them, slightly sickened by the thick waves of stale cigarette smoke, so thick you could see them, especially around the lights that hung above the pool tables in cracked orange lampshades. The place was a bit of a kip, but it didn't matter, because there was a deadly atmosphere.

'They said to tell youse they had to go on and to follow them up,' we were told by a girl who looked up at us from under her baseball cap, flicking her ashes on the ground well clear of her immaculate white runners.

'Nice of them to wait for us,' Brenda snapped.

'They couldn't, there were pigs parked right in the village.'

'Fucking nice one. Now, how are we going to get our

drink?' Emma demanded of the night air angrily as soon as we were outside.

I took long deep breaths; I'd been suffocating in there.

'We'll just have to wait to sit on a wall and ask anyone we see to go into the offo for us,' Brenda said, pissed off, but resigned to the calamity.

'Oh for fuck sake, we'll be here all night.'

'At least it's still early,' I offered, trying to lighten the mood.

'Yeah, well, if everyone else hadn't been so fucking early we wouldn't have this fucking problem,' Brenda muttered venomously from behind a cloud of smoke.

They were both in filthy moods and I decided silence would be the best policy.

We sat on a wall, around the corner from the offo so that they wouldn't see us from the window and cop what was going on. There wasn't a pig in sight, and I didn't know if that made them feel better or worse. We sat, them with cigarettes, lowered to the other side of the wall every time a passer-by approached in case it was someone the oul pair knew, and quickly reclaimed if it was someone suitable for the offo, whereupon they'd jump up, approach them, and the pleading would commence. 'Ah, go on, it won't take a minute, please go in for us, please, please.'

Five potentials and no luck. We were majorly pissed off and despairing. Emma paced up and down the path, her eyes peeled on the horizon. Forward and back and forward and back. Forward again. She paused and then ran back excitedly.

'Oh my God, I've just seen Paul walking into the newsagent.'

Brenda jumped up.

'Show us.'

They ran down the road to stare at the shop in the distance and ran back again.

'He's just come out and he's walking down this way,' they told me, full of jittery anticipation.

'Why don't you ask him to go to the offo for us?' I suggested.

'Ask Paul, fucking scarlet, no way, anyway he never goes to the offo for anyone,' Emma explained distractedly, furtively looking to see how close he was. 'Here he is, you ask him.'

They sat on the wall and averted their eyes. I looked down the road and saw a blurred shadowy dot swim into focus in the form of one of the most beautiful fellas I'd ever seen, with the most arrogant swagger I've yet come across. Long thick black curly hair and big brown eyes and the most gorgeous face. Strong cheekbones and flawless skin. He was wearing a black leather coat that came to his knees and a blue shirt and red jeans, and loads of necklaces and two silver earrings in each ear. But it didn't look too much on him, it all looked just right on him, perfect. Not that it would have mattered to me otherwise, because this prototype rock star made flesh, the local hero, was unattainable, and even if he wasn't, I knew he'd be way out of my range. I found it difficult enough handling fourteen-year-old girls, never mind eighteen-year-old idols. But I had to walk up to him on the street and talk to him. He had almost reached me.

'Will you go to the offo for us?'

He didn't hear me and passed right by. Not surprisingly, my throat was so tight my voice sounded like a whispered mumble, and he looked spaced out as if he saw nothing, me or no-one. I was almost relieved. But Emma gave me a filthy look, and I knew I had to do better than that.

'Do you mind, I was talking to you,' I shouted at his retreating back.

He swung around, startled, to see me, tongue-tied, and Emma and Brenda, sitting on the wall, their faces buried in their hands, and by the sounds that were lowly emanating from them, trying to control their laughter.

'You talking to me?'

'Yeah, you walked straight past us.'

'Well, I didn't hear you.' He walked back. He wasn't exactly apologetic, but at least he wasn't angry, or pissed off. Emma and Brenda managed to shut up completely and look up, but they didn't speak.

'So what did you want?'

He was being nice, and looking at me like he was interested in what I was saying. This wouldn't be so bad.

I relaxed and smiled. 'We need someone to go to the offo for us.'

'I don't know, I'd have to think about it. I wouldn't mind going for a good-looking girl like yourself, but I'd have to take a look at the other two sitting there breaking their arses laughing.'

They burst out in a fresh fit. 'What are you on?' Emma asked, looking directly at him.

'On? I'm on nothing. Well, I might have taken

something earlier on, but that was then, and this is now. So, who are youse?' he asked, looking at me.

I began to speak, but Emma cut in on me loudly, and my voice died away.

'I'm, Emma, this is Brenda, and we're from Greenmeadows. That's my friend, Cassandra, from school, she's staying over with me. She lives in Ashford.' Ashford with a touch of derision.

He looked at me with wonder and pity.

'Are you loaded or what?'

'Yes she is, she lives in a bleeding mansion.'

'Shut up, will you, she can talk for herself,' he commanded, still looking at me. I glanced over at Emma. 'So what are you doing out here, then?'

'Going drinking with Emma and her friends.'

'Yeah? Have you been coming out here long?'

'No, this is my second night. So will you go to the offo for us?'

'I suppose I'll have to. What do youse want?'

'Emma'll tell you.'

She stepped forward with the money clenched in her fist. 'Three flagons.'

'That all?'

'We have to go home tonight.'

'Fair enough. That's easy to remember, anyway.' He went off.

They laughed with glee as soon as he'd turned the corner. 'I don't believe it, I don't fucking believe it,' Emma said, grabbing Brenda's arm.

'I know. Now shut up in case he hears you.'

We waited quietly, the other two whispering to each

other once in a while and not looking once in my direction. I felt as if I was being punished for Paul's attention. But I couldn't help that.

He returned with two plastic bags. 'There youse go. Happy now?'

I lingered in the shadows while Emma and Brenda stepped forward with profuse thanks and respectful adulation. They put the bags into Brenda's big PE bag.

'Where are youse off to?'

Emma described the spot in detail for him. Same place we were in last week.

'I know it, yeah. I used to drink there myself, many moons ago. I might see youse down there later. How long'll youse be there?'

With delight, they told him, and decorously begged him, as far as they dared, to come down whenever he could make it.

'I'll see you later, then,' he said, touching me on the arm before he left.

When he was out of sight Emma and Brenda broke into excited speculation.

'Tell me this, Brenda, do I or do I not have a chance with him?'

'Of course you do, I saw the way he was looking at you.'

'But he was looking at her more than he was looking at me.'

'Well, he would have been looking at you if she hadn't been there.'

'Well, if it hadn't been for me, youse wouldn't have been talking to him at all.' I was incredulous.

'Only because we didn't have the cheek to walk up to him in the street,' Brenda countered. 'Come on, let's go.'

I walked beside them down the street, wondering how to recover the ground I'd lost. It was only natural that they were upset. The fella Emma'd fancied for years had talked to me more than her, and it had been me he said he'd see later. But I'd never even considered going near anyone Emma liked, never mind someone like Paul that I'd be afraid to go near anyway.

'D'you think he's good looking?' Emma asked, casually enough, but with an edge.

So what's the right answer, Cassandra? Think, Cassandra, think. 'Oh he is, yeah, but he's not my type.'

'Excuse me,' Brenda said scornfully. 'Not good enough for you, is he?'

From bad to worse. 'It's not that at all,' I said wretchedly. 'I think he's a ride, of course I do, but Emma's mad into him, and I wouldn't want youse to think I'd deliberately do anything to interfere with her chances with him.'

Emma smiled triumphantly. 'I know you wouldn't.'

Peace was restored, and we hurried on, out of the village and down to the community centre.

'Not a word to anyone,' Emma cautioned, as we approached. 'The last thing we need is a crowd of young ones all over Paul if and when he gets here.' We promised to keep our mouths shut, and we squeezed through the fence where there was a railing missing.

CHAPTER 11

We reached the others, and shouted greetings all round as we sank to the ground. Everyone was in good humour, sitting around in groups, chatting away and singing. Some people were in real hyper moods, shouting and jumping around the place, going into stitches when they tripped against trees and fell over; except when they spilt some drink.

Michelle ran over to us, clutching a can. She seemed to be quite drunk already.

'I think we can trust Michelle,' Emma said, smiling slyly as she approached us. 'Alright, Michelle, you'll never guess what.'

She sat down beside us. 'What? You look pleased with yourself. Howya, Cassandra.'

'Paul said he might be coming down here to see me later on.'

'Paul? What Paul?'

'*The* Paul.'

'Not Paul, Mick's brother?'

'Who else?'

'Yeah, right, fuck off.'

'No, he is coming, I swear.'

The other two explained with glee, while Michelle's

expression changed from incredulity to worried concern. I couldn't figure out whether it was the drink, or whether she was genuinely horrified.

'I wouldn't go near him if I were you. He's probably only after his hole.'

'Thanks a lot.'

'It's got nothing to do with you, it'd be the same if it was anyone else. He's an awful gobshite. He lives in my estate, I know what he's like. My brother told me. He's on all kinds of drugs.'

'You're a fine one to talk, you smoke as much blow as the rest of us.'

'Blow's nothing. I'm not talking about blow, I'm talking about the hard stuff. Stay well away from him.'

'Emma told me loads of youse drop Es and stuff when youse go to raves in town,' I offered.

'Not loads of us, Cassandra. The one time I did, I never felt worse in my life after. And God only knows what Paul's on. I know a girl that went out with him, lovely girl, about his age, and beautiful looking, and she says to me, when she broke it off with him a week later, she says to me, "Paul thinks he's the next Jim Morrison, only with him, instead of being interested in sex, drugs, rock'n'roll and being a bastard, he's only interested in sex, drugs and being a bastard".'

Emma and Brenda broke their holes laughing.

'Do you not think that's just a little bit over the top?'

She shook her head in exasperation. 'Laugh as much as youse want, for all I care, but I'm telling you, he's a prick.'

'Obviously. I thought you liked him?' Emma said.

'Oh, Emma, it's a pity I haven't had a good talk to you

in a long time, or I might have saved you this. God, I need a drink now, after that.' Michelle threw away her empty can and got up to get another one.

'Did you bring the blow with you?' Emma asked Brenda.

'No, we said we'd save it for tomorrow night, remember?'

A look of conspiracy passed between them. 'Oh yeah.'

Michelle returned with two cans. She sat down, put one beside her and opened the other one.

'I'm down to my last two cans now. Listen, Casssandra, I don't want to freak you out or anything, but you know the way Kev's mad into you?'

'Yeah . . ?'

'Well, he knows you're here, he saw you and Emma getting off the bus, only he was at work, he works in the newsagent's across the road from the bus stop. And he was going on about you when I went in to buy smokes, saying he'd try to get up here later to see you if he was finished work early enough. Now I told him you weren't interested, but he said he wouldn't believe it from me and that he'd come up anyway.'

'Oh my God, what'll I do?'

'Nothing. Sit back and enjoy yourself. And if he does show up, which he probably won't, just tell him you're not interested.'

My nerves went into overload. I sat where I was, and I drank and drank, trying to dispel all negative emotions so I could relax and enjoy the night and the good company.

Soon I was buzzing and relaxed, chatting away to anyone and everyone, told Emma, I like you Emma, you're my friend, and you are going to get Paul, and it'll work out great, and I love you too, Brenda, are you my friend too? Yes, Cassandra, I'm your friend, and I am too. All of us on an equal buzz, laughing, sociable and friendly. And you too, Michelle, you're a really nice person as well. I smiled to the world, benevolent and gregarious, drinking from my emptying flagon, my gaze lighting on the raver fellas. Like Kev. Oh Holy Fuck, Kev might be coming, and the stabbing pain at the pit of my stomach again, oh, quick, more drink, look, I can knock it back like water now, Emma. A bemused throw away of a smile from eyes with the simpleton-child haze of alcohol, my God, Emma must really be locked, and so must I, to be thinking like that, though I would never mean that Emma's eyes are really like a simpleton child's, just when she's locked, like now, like me. Only I'm getting more locked than she is, I can tell, though she's finished her flagon and I'm not. Not yet, nearly. Emma throws her bottle away and it nearly hits someone, but it doesn't. Jesus Christ, there's someone puking their guts up beside me.

'Get up, quick, Cassandra.'

Emma's voice, her and Brenda pulling me to my feet. Look, I can't even stand up properly, the rest of me is as light as my head, or is it heavy, because I can't stay up as we move away, well away from the puke, where we can't see or smell it, that's what they're saying, anyway, I can't smell anything, and I'm too busy looking at my feet, to make sure they're going one foot forward at a time on clear ground. Emma lets go of me to sit down, and I fall forward, but I can't feel it, dropping my bottle, but it has the lid on, I know I put the lid on, just before the puker

116

came, because I know I was thinking, look, here's Emma
throwing hers away and I've to put the lid on mine,
because I can't drink anymore yet because I'm bursting to
go to the toilet and I don't like to interrupt the others'
conversation to get someone to go with me, not just yet,
because they're having such a good time. But I mustn't
have put the lid on, because Brenda's saying it's all gone,
you've spilt the rest of it. And Emma's saying that's right,
and you can't drink anymore, thank God we've two hours
before we have to go home because you're too fucking
locked. I'll fucking kill you if we're snared. I'm bursting to
go to the toilet, Emma. Here, I'll go with you. Thanks
Michelle, and she leads me by the arm, and I piss happily
away, no hang-ups this time about people seeing me,
though I know they can't, Michelle's looking out for me,
I'm more locked than last week, or I was, because my
coordination is better after pissing, only the buzz is going
away, and I'm still heavy, or is it light, and my mind and
senses are dulled, thanks be to fuck, because there's Kev
standing there, about ten yards away shouting howya, are
you locked? and Michelle's gripping my arm, tightly and
supportively, and I say Hi, bye, I've nothing to say to you,
smile with relief, and walk on back to the others, say to
Michelle, and Emma, and Brenda, do youse think he got
the message, and we sit down, and Michelle says
doubtfully, I don't think he heard a word you said, we
were too far away and you were a bit quiet, by the look on
his face, he didn't hear a word you said. Shooting pains
again, no drink to pacify them with. Buzz going away,
senses slightly alive again, but still an overall numbing of
consciousness, thank God. Desperate to go to the toilet

117

again. No, not yet. Feel my mind, body and soul engulfed by the need to piss, alright, where's Michelle, over there talking to someone.

'Emma, I have to go to the bog.'

'Yeah, me too, come on.'

I let her go first, though my sides are splitting, and I'm doubled over.

There's Kev's friend. 'You can't go in there.'

'No, I wanted to talk to you.'

I can't hold it any longer or I'll piss in my knickers.

'Yeah? What do you want?'

Some shouting beyond. I'm distracted by the noise, the fear someone might walk in on Emma, and my kidneys. He says something, I can't hear him, he says it again, will I go off with Kev tonight. Scrawny little thing, looks about ten, probably because he's been chain-smoking since he was about five.

'No,' I say.

Then he says something else, repeats it, says it again, says something else and something else. My brain can't make it out.

'Yes,' I say. 'No,' 'I don't know, what are you saying?'

Again, and again and he goes off happy.

'Wait,' I call, 'what did I say?' and he doesn't hear me, and I forget all about it because Emma emerges and I can piss at last.

Much better now, more lucid, Emma takes my arm.

'Paul never came.'

'How late is it?'

'Late. Eleven o'clock. One hour to sober up.'

'Have you any idea where he is?'

'He might be at the chipper or in the pub.'

'Let's go see then.'

Emma is delighted, and we set off with Brenda. Michelle shaking her head in exasperated resignation. Thank God I don't see Kev anymore.

We go, and sit down from the chipper, he's not there, and the pub is across the road and down a bit. We'd see him come out. Half-eleven, no sign of him. Brenda's getting impatient, goes and buys some chips, I sit supportively with Emma. Quarter to twelve, Brenda throws her greasy brown paper chip bag away, and we watch it bounce up and down in the wind, which is either speeding up now, or we didn't notice it before. My head is clear, but I feel so tired, so I'm glad of the wind, it's waking me up.

'We'd better head, Emma.'

'Just another minute.'

Emma sat there, staring down the road. Silently she passed me mints to suck and some to Brenda.

'We'll be late, Emma. My mam'll kill me.'

'A few minutes won't matter.'

'Well it does to me. And he's not coming, he's probably somewhere else.'

Emma ignored her. Ten to twelve, I looked down the road. Emma jumped up. 'There he is now, coming out of the pub.'

They lit up smokes and pretended to be just lounging around casually.

'What are youse doing here?'

'Just dossing.'

'Oh right. I couldn't get down to youse, I had to meet the lads for a pint. Band business, you know.'

Emma was thrilled. 'I know what you mean, yeah.'

'So, what's happening?'

'Oh, nothing much.' She looked to Brenda for encouragement, and Brenda nodded back. 'Brenda's got a free gaff tomorrow night. Her oul pair are going down the bog and bringing the kids with them. So, we're going to have a quiet night of it, no mad party, just us and a few tinnies.'

'Yeah? Sounds deadly. Just yourselves, is it?' He looked at us, and me.

They nodded, but I didn't know what to do, this was the first I'd heard of it.

'Will you still be here then?'

Brenda indicated to me to say yeah, and I said yeah. I was pleased, it sounded cool. That must have been what they were talking about earlier on. I only hoped my parents would allow me to stay over two nights in a row, and I'd make sure Emma had every opportunity with him, even though he was still looking at me and not her.

'Nice one. I'll see youse then.'

He studied the address, written in my eyeliner on the inside of an empty cigarette packet, before shoving it in his pocket and setting off down the road. I was horrified to see how much of my eyeliner had been used up, but I said nothing, not wanting to taint the general jubilation.

'It'd be better if you didn't come tomorrow night. You don't mind, do you?'

Hurt and surprise. They were staring at me.

'Well, I was looking forward to it. You did invite me.'

Brenda took up where Emma had left off, not that it

120

made any difference who spoke. They both took the same line.

'Yes, but that was in front of Paul, because he wants you to be there. And she wouldn't stand a chance with him with you around. You don't want that, do you?'

I could understand the logic, and upset as I was, I knew that the right thing would be not to go. But if they were asking such a favour, why weren't they being nicer, and more apologetic, instead of hostile, almost as if they were striking military bargains with the enemy?

My blood turned cold. I wanted them to be my friends. They were my friends, weren't they?

'I suppose it'd be for the best if I didn't come, alright.'

They were satisfied with that, though they still looked at me with scorn, I thought, scorn that I could be pushed so far and still be compliant, despising me for it, storing it up for future reference. And I was chilled through, right beyond the bone where the biting wind couldn't reach, a bitter chill that remained with me, undiminished by the silent frenzied run home because we were so late or the burning wrath of Emma's mam.

'I was worried sick about youse.'

'Cassandra felt sick, Mam, and we had to sit with her until she was able to walk.'

'You look very pale alright. I hope youse weren't drinking.'

'No, Mam.'

'Youse should have rung me and I would have come and got youse in the car instead of the poor child walking home in the cold. Were youse in Michelle's till this hour?'

'No, her friend's, and we're only fifteen minutes late, it wasn't worth getting you out for that.'

'Do you hear that now? I wish you were that concerned about me more often.'

'Shut up, Mam.'

But everything was fine with her now that we were back safe and sound. We went up to bed, her continuing to voice concern about my health. Alone with Emma again, I felt a bit awkward, but she was nice enough, if quiet and a little distant. She fell asleep immediately. And no snoring. I was surprised. But I couldn't sleep, even without that irritant. I lay awake, trying to wrap myself completely in the blanket to shield myself from the draughts coming at me from the window and the door, but even still I lay there chilled, staring at the crack of light coming underneath the door. Miserable, and desolate, too drained to torture myself or even to figure out if that was a good or a bad thing.

Just misery and desolation.

CHAPTER 12

Emma woke up late the following morning and was still very quiet and distant.

'Are you alright?' I asked her.

'Yeah, I'm fine. I just have a headache.'

We went down for breakfast. Emma's mam kept asking her what her plans for the day were. 'Don't forget you have to fit your homework in somewhere. Or there'll be no staying over with Brenda tonight.'

'I know, I'll do it when Cassandra's gone home.'

'When are you heading, love? There's no rush or anything, but I want to get her time-table for the day sorted out, even though the day's half gone at this stage, it's almost twelve already.'

'I'll go as soon as I'm finished breakfast.'

'Are you sure? You don't have to leave that early, sure she doesn't Emma?'

I looked at Emma, who didn't seem to mind one way or the other, but then, she had a headache.

'No, like I have some things to do at home anyway.'

'Me and Brenda'll walk you to the bus stop. I'll just go and ring her now.' She picked up the phone and arranged for Brenda to come over in a few minutes.

'My Emma's really hitting the books these days. I was

delighted with the "B" she got in the maths test last week, that's why I'm letting her have two nights out this weekend as a special treat.'

'I see.' What maths test?

Emma looked at me warningly. I sat there, playing with my toast. I hadn't eaten anything.

'Well, I'll leave youse to it, girls.' She left the room and went upstairs.

'What maths test?'

'You know, the homework we got last week where you had to do it out on the handouts? Well, I marked most of them right and wrote "Good Work Emma, B," and the date at the end.'

'And you got away with it?'

'Of course I did. That stupid bitch wouldn't know the difference.'

Silence again.

'Are you sure you're alright?'

'Yeah, I'm just a bit nervous about tonight, that's all.'

The bell rang and Emma ran to let Brenda in. 'Sure you haven't even eaten anything yet,' she said.

I looked at the cold toast. 'I'm not hungry.'

'She never eats anything anyway, you should see her in school, just picking at her lunch.'

'You should eat more, you're way too skinny.'

'All the supermodels and actresses are much skinnier than me, and everyone thinks they're gorgeous,' I answered defensively. I wasn't that thin, and anyway I did eat, just not lately, because I'd been upset.

'Well, I read somewhere that they're all forty per cent

underweight, and they're all anorexic as well. Aren't they, Brenda?'

'Yeah, the cameras make them look half-a-stone fatter or something, so they have to be that much thinner than we think they are. And they put all sorts of make-up onto them to make them better looking, so I wouldn't say a lot of them are good-looking at all in real life, just tall and skinny.'

'Speak for yourself, I wouldn't mind looking like one,' Emma said, pinching the fat on her face with disgust; 'All the same, you could do with a few pounds here and there, Cassandra. Then you wouldn't look so much like the walking dead, and your eyes'd look smaller.'

'Thanks a lot,' I said, trying to sound indignant rather than heartbroken.

'I didn't mean it like that. Friends should be able to say these things to one another for their own good without the other one getting their knickers in a knot about it.' She was being a bit nicer now than she'd been earlier on, but it still hurt.

I went upstairs to get my bag, and said goodbye to Emma's mam. 'I'll see you soon, love. Don't forget you're welcome here any time.'

Yes, but would Emma want me back? Of course she would.

We walked to the bus stop, the other two keeping a preoccupied silence.

'Bye Cassandra, I'll tell you all about it in school on Monday. And don't mind me, I'm just narky as fuck because I'm shitting it about tonight,' Emma said.

I smiled back at her, relieved.

'I know, and don't worry about it, everything'll work out fine.'

I got on the bus, and waved until they were out of sight.

I hoped and hoped Emma would get to go out with Paul, because surely that would put her in better form. The best I could do was wish with all my heart that everything worked out tonight.

Half-past five, the time was getting closer now, hastily scribble off the last of the French. I pictured her getting out of the shower and painstakingly combing out her hair, everything had to be perfect. Quarter-past six, closer again. Oh Emma!

I went down to eat my dinner, but I couldn't eat a lot of it.

'Are you not starving?'

'No, well I'm a bit sick.'

'Oh God, probably a bit of a bug.'

'Yeah.'

Emma was sitting in her room now, already dressed, hair still damp, with Brenda meticulously applying make-up. I drank a cup of coffee. Emma was probably sipping a cup right now, before fixing her hair.

'That film you wanted to see's starting now.'

Seven o'clock, they'd be leaving soon.

'This early?'

'Yeah.'

I went and sat in front of the screen. But that's my problem with television. If there's something on my mind, then I don't take it in. I just sit there, ten thousand things passing through my head, watching the pictures go by without seeing them. It's not dark yet. Another cup of coffee which I can't drink, time goes on, I doze off. Big crash and I wake up. There's been a car crash, I hate car crashes in films, I've seen too many. It's dark now, Emma's probably in Brenda's house now, getting locked, Paul's there, or on his way.

My mum looks in. 'If you're tired, go to bed.'

And I go up, and fall asleep, still hoping everything's going well. And wake up next morning, still hoping everything went well, is going well, will go well.

CHAPTER 13

I was in school early Monday morning, on the offchance Emma'd be in early. She wasn't. She was late. But she gave me a look of pure joy, so I knew she'd met Paul. Quick note: 'Met Paul, Saturday night, Sunday, and tonight. Why didn't you tell me you were going with Kev?'

My blood ran cold and I wrote back shakily, like a spider, barely touching the page, barely making a mark. 'I'm not. What do you mean?'

'He's told everyone,' she whispered. 'Says you told his friend you would on Saturday night. I said you hadn't told me, but he says you are and he wants your phone number.'

That was all we could manage. My mind swirled frantically. I vaguely remembered talking to his friend, but couldn't for the life of me remember what he'd said or what I'd said. But surely I'd never be so drunk as to say yes to Kev. I had to talk to Emma. After the class, we hurried out and into a quiet corner.

'Emma, you have to tell him I'm not going with him.'

'I don't blame you, I'll tell him this evening. Will I see him this evening? Yes, definitely, he'll be in Johnny's, he told me he'd be there.'

'What made him think I was going with him?'

'Your man, Shane, says you said yes when he asked you.'

'I didn't.'

'I believe you. Paul said it was disgusting, you meeting Kev in the first place, he's glad it wasn't me, because I'm the one he was with. He'd never have been with me if I'd been with Kev.'

We were late for class, so we had to go in. To think of a misunderstanding as big as that, and Paul despising me completely now. Emma didn't, but there was something condescending in her attitude that hadn't been there before. But I had never seen her in such a euphoric mood before either. I just walked on eggshells around her with cowed heart, hoping she'd come back to earth soon.

She was still the same on Tuesday, only higher, because Paul had asked her to go with him.

'He is so nice to me, Cassandra,' she said at lunchtime as we sheltered from the rain by a classroom radiator. 'And he is such a good shift.'

'Did you talk to Kev?' There, the question I'd been afraid to ask all morning. Emma had been busy anyway trying to get as much homework as possible done between classes and at little break so she'd be free to see Paul again tonight. She was just having a quick break now to eat her lunch.

'Yeah. It's cool.'

'What did he say?'

'That it was probably a good thing, seeing as you were the most frigid person he'd ever met.' She looked at me reprovingly.

'How embarrassing.'

'Well it was, seeing as he said it out loud in Johnny's, and everybody heard him, including Paul. But you'll be alright, they'll forget soon enough.'

All yesterday and today I'd felt like a whipped dog. Now I felt like a whipped dog that had been shot to pieces. Emma was looking worried.

'Are you alright, Cassandra? You're not going to *cry*, are you?' There was enough scorn in her tone for me to pull myself together.

'And did you stick up for me?'

'Of course I did. Now, don't kill me for this, I had to say something, I said, "well what did you expect, it was her first time with anyone." '

'Oh Emma, how could you? You promised me you'd never say that to anyone.'

'Well I thought it'd help.'

'Did it?'

'I don't know, because Michelle pulled me outside and said she'd bate me if I said another word, and not to bother coming near her again, so it's me you should be feeling sorry for, not yourself.' She finished with a touch of martyrdom.

'What did Paul say?'

'That he was glad he didn't have a frigid girlfriend, but you wouldn't mind him, he's scarlet enough as it is about going with a fourteen-year-old.'

So Paul hated me and everyone hated me. Wasn't that always the way?

'Back in a minute.' I picked up my bag and walked away, ignoring Emma's concerned pleas of 'Cassandra, come back here, don't go.'

I walked to the least-used toilets, locked myself in, and cried my eyes out, standing against the wall because there wasn't even a toilet seat for me to sit on. Soundlessly, so no one'd hear me. An old trick from primary school. Seems like I was using a lot of old tricks lately.

The bell rang for class. I took my hands down from my face to let the swelling go down (rubbing only makes it worse) and waited for the toilets to empty. Then I wetted a mound of dry toilet roll with cold water, trying not to put my hand in the sink because it was all clogged up with decomposing toilet roll and dirty grey water. I applied my toilet roll to my eyes. I hate looking at myself in toilet mirrors; it always makes my skin look awful, yellowy and unhealthy and blotchy. Especially today, with puffy little red eyes. Not bad two minutes later, but still not perfect, and I really had to go. So I let my hair down, shook it forward, and hung my head. Better.

'Sorry I'm late.' I sat down beside Emma. She'd looked ill at ease and preoccupied as I walked past the window on my way in, but a relieved smile broke out all over her face as I walked in, a warm smile that eased my heart.

'What happened to you? I was worried sick.'

I'd always have Emma. She mightn't be perfect, but I'd always have her.

And she was nice all that day, and the next day, which was Wednesday, our half-day, and she was going to spend the whole day with Paul.

'An "A" in an English essay,' she explained slyly in Religion.

'Does your mam know about Paul?'

'No she doesn't, she'd kill me.'

'Cassandra and Emma, you are both getting far too chatty for your own good. I've had a lot of complaints about you from the other teachers. Time to separate.'

And so I was left on my own while Emma was put at an empty desk just in front of Linda and Natasha. If they didn't look as pissed-off as they would have had it been me, they didn't look exactly thrilled either.

'Oh, well, never mind,' said Emma as we walked to the bus stop, resigned to the break-up, if unhappy about it. 'See you tomorrow.'

But I didn't see Emma the next day. Instead I got a phone call to say she was going on the hop so she could spend the day with Paul. I didn't see her the next day either, or that weekend.

School was lonely without her. I moped around, spending breaks doing homework and reading and stuff. I ate with Sinéad and Tessa, explaining that Emma was on the hop, expecting condemnation, but instead getting a politely concealed expression of disgust.

I spent the days and nights in sorrow over my loss of face in Kilmore. I prayed that it would die down so I could go out there again soon. Certainly while Emma was going out with Paul, I couldn't go out with her as he hated me too. Not that I wanted them to break up. It would upset Emma too much. But they weren't all laughing at me. It would mainly be the fellas. Michelle didn't hate me, or Brenda, it would just be too embarrassing to face them all. Then there was Jane, I remembered her fondly, and Mick and Brian, but they probably didn't remember me. I wished my life had been different, that I'd grown up in

Kilmore and been in the same class at school as Emma and Brenda and Jane and Michelle and all those others, including the fellas, because they wouldn't be laughing at me now. I'd be just as good as all the other girls. Okay, Emma wouldn't be in my class anymore, but I'd still see her at the weekends. I wouldn't have a nice house or have known Aisling, but they'd have been worth giving up. If only. Then I wouldn't be depressed all the time, or worrying about Emma's relationship with Paul. For her sake, I hoped he wasn't the bastard Michelle said he was, but then, she wasn't talking to Emma now because she thought Emma had been mean to me, and, flattering as that was, it showed her judgement wasn't exactly spot on.

Monday came and went without Emma. A long-awaited letter from Aisling in America arrived. She loved it and had lots of new friends, her life was described in detail. I brought it to school, and showed it to Sinéad and Tessa, who'd been asking for her only last week. As we discussed it, I realised how little I'd spoken to them this year, which was a pity, because they weren't that bad to talk to really. I wrote back to Aisling, talking positively about Emma and Kilmore, wanting to concentrate on the good rather than the bad.

Another phonecall from Emma to say she wouldn't be in tomorrow. 'You'd better come back to school soon. It's getting risky.'

'I know, what have you been telling them?'

'I say I haven't heard from you, so you must be really sick, and the teachers laugh and say, "She must be if she's not on the phone gassing to you," and everybody laughs.'

'Good, hold on a minute.' She put down the phone and shouted, 'I'll be finished in a minute. I'm just checking some homework with Cassandra . . . I have to go now, bye.' She hung up.

She rang again on Tuesday night, crying her eyes out, Paul had another girlfriend, an eighteen-year-old from another town. She'd told her mam the exam pressure was too much for her especially on top of her ' 'flu', which was why she was upset, and she was having a few days off. She'd persuaded her mam not to ring the school herself, just to let her ring Cassandra.

'I'm really really sorry.'

'So am I.'

I didn't hear from her again. I rang, but her mam said she was in bed and wouldn't be in till Monday.

'Tell me this, love, how is Emma really getting on in school?'

She sounded like she was worried sick, and I felt guilt about all the lies she'd been fed. Emma wasn't that bright, but she'd be alright if she worked.

'She's a bit overwhelmed by everything, and I think she feels pressured because the others are all brainy and she feels she can't live up to them.'

That was true anyway, for her and me both.

'The poor girl, no wonder she's so upset. She's been working so hard, down at the library in the village and everything.'

So that was where she said she was all the time. This conversation made me feel really bad. I couldn't stand it any longer.

'I have to go now, would you tell Emma I was asking for her and I'll see her on Monday.'

CHAPTER 14

Emma was late to school on Monday. I hadn't seen her in a while, or talked to her since the break-up, and I was shocked to see how bad she looked. She had broken out in spots, and there were big shadows under her eyes, and her make-up was thicker than usual. Her 'flu must have been worse than I had thought.

She handed in a note from her mam excusing her absence; I didn't know if it was semi-real or forged, but it was accepted with a brief 'hope you're feeling better now'. I tried to catch her eye, but she looked and walked straight past me.

We weren't in the same classes after that, but when I searched the school for her at little break, I couldn't find her. Sinéad told me that she had seen her in a cloakroom with Linda and Natasha, having an intense conversation. I couldn't believe it. She hated them, and always had. But it was true. She walked into the room with them, taking care not to look my way. They stuck close together, disappearing in a flash after classes, unlocatable at lunch-time. By the end of the day, I knew they were ignoring me.

The next day, I was late for class, having had to force myself to get there at all. Emma was there, looking stoned. She must have been smoking blow before coming to school. If she was depressed enough to be smoking blow in the mornings, why would she bother coming in at all? Something was seriously wrong. Maybe it was to do with her parents, and she was too scared shitless to go on the hop in case she was caught and it made things worse. That could be it. Going on the hop hadn't bothered her before. She needed me, she wasn't really ignoring me. She was just too upset.

But between classes and at little break they were up and away in a flash again. And when I looked over during class, Emma and Linda looked away, and Natasha stared back at me with pure disgust and disdain.

Not only that, but by little break, I was beginning to sense the cold looks directed at me from everywhere, and I was sure people were talking about me behind my back. It was awful. I spent the break on my own in the cloakroom, sitting on the ground against the hot pipes, a load of grey gabardines looped away from me through the strap of my bag. I tried not to look at my bag because Emma had written her name all over it in thick marker. What was going on, why did Emma hate me all of a sudden?

When the break was over, I counted the minutes it would take for the teacher to get to the classroom so I wouldn't have to go in before her. But she was late, and I wasn't even spared that. Things were worse now. There was a silence when I entered, and then the hum of voices rose again, all the clusters of pairs and cliques taking care to focus their eyes on anything and everything but me, but still, even though I looked at my desk, and examined my book, and my blue plastic biro with full attention, I couldn't help but notice the cold and curious glances towards me. I sat there, afraid even to look round at Sinéad and Tessa because I had no idea what they thought, and if they disliked me as much as everyone else seemed to, then I'd probably start crying, right here and now, and I couldn't bear that. Much better to put on a show of not being affected by any of this.

Lunchtime I went and sat outside, safe from the view of the other girls, it was too cold and windy for them, thank God it wasn't raining. And there was some shelter, sitting between the small grey concrete boiler house and the block of outdoor toilets on the cement ground. The sort of place you could have a smoke safe enough if you weren't too chicken.

Don't mind them, I thought, if they're this mean and all hate you for nothing, even Emma, they're not worth knowing. Not worth thinking about, not worth getting upset about. But my arguments resounded hollowly in my head. I couldn't work out why this was happening, because my mind didn't dare think about it, except from a distance, for fear of aggravating the pressure in my stomach, and the pounding of my heart that I could almost see, moving up and down, forwards and backwards, from side to side, like a shipwrecked sailor battered against the rocks in a thundering storm, hoping that the wind will die down, knowing he'll die if it doesn't.

Fifteen minutes then five minutes, how can it only be five minutes now? Time, time to head back, slowly, throwing my lunch in the bin, not looking at it, because the sight of it revolts me, unobtrusively in case a teacher comments on the waste and what the starving in the third world would do for that food. Very good, Cassandra, you think of everything, except what's important, you're pretty fucked there, aren't you?

Back in, sit in silence, frequent trips to the toilets in between classes so you don't have to wait alone outside the next class. All those eyes and Emma's. Emma's eyes. To the toilet after school to wait until everyone else has left. I used to do this every day in primary school. Will I have to do it every day for the rest of my life? Shut up, you stupid bitch. No it's alright, I'm far too drained for tears anyway.

Home again.

'I'm back.'

'How was school?'

'Fine.'

'Was Emma in today?'

Too painful to say anything, nothing they can do anyway. 'Yeah.'

'Are you alright? You look a bit sick. I hope you're not coming down with Emma's 'flu.'

'No, I'm just a bit tired.'

I'd love a few days in bed, but I have to go in tomorrow and talk to Emma, otherwise I'll never have the guts to do it. Ring her. Ring her later. She'll be in tonight, after nine or so. She'll have to talk to you, then. Do your homework now, so you can work out what to say to her. I rush it off quickly, most of it's wrong, but I don't care. Eat your dinner, I can actually eat it, now that I'm going to sort it all out in two hours' time. Just say to her, what's wrong, did I do something on you? That'd do.

In a nice apologetic way so she won't hang up on you.

Nine o'clock. Hands shaking. Pick up the phone beside the water-bed in my parents' bedroom and press the wrong numbers. Go to the door and check no-one can hear me. Lock it, turn the key with the flowery keyring. Back on to the water-bed and the blue duvet with violet flowers that match the keyring. Sit there until the water stills and settles. Pick up the phone again. This time I don't press some of the numbers properly so they don't go through. Cop on, you dopey bitch. Again. Right numbers, ringing. I can't do this, hang it up, no, yes, too late.

'Hello.' Emma's mam.

'Hello.'

She can't hear me. She says 'Hello,' again.

'Hello, is Emma there please?'

'Is that Cassandra?'

She's pleased to hear me, talk about relief.

'Yeah.'

'How are you getting on?'

'Fine.'

'That's good, I'll get her for you now.'

She leaves the phone down, opens the door, calls out 'Emma, phone.' Whispers. Closes the door behind her. Comes back into the room a few minutes later.

'I'm sorry love, she's not here, I thought she was, but she's not.'

She's lying, the embarrassment and awkwardness seeps through her voice, like me when I'm talking to her about Emma. We've got something in common, surprisingly.

Emma must have put her up to this. Nothing I can do about it, except hope she doesn't end up hating me too.

'Okay, bye.'

'Bye.'

CHAPTER 15

Bedtime. Sleeplessness, sadness, anger, self-hatred, hopelessness, frustration, tears. Too much time on my hands to torment myself, but no brains to make sense of what is happening, or to know what to do. Papers, television, leaflets, guidance classes in school. They all said ask for help if you need it. There are people you can talk to, your parents, teachers, the Samaritans. In primary school it had made me feel worse. Now I wouldn't even consider it. How embarrassing. They'd all think I was some kind of fucking eejit. A paranoid social reject. It'd be one thing if I said something like, 'My parents were killed in a car crash last week and I was gang-raped on the way home from the funeral. Help me.' But to open my mouth and say, 'They all hate me and are talking about me behind my back and in front of it too.' The scorn for someone with such a problem intensified by the fact that she'd actually thought it important enough to bother them about it. 'So? What do you expect us to do about it? You're a big girl now. You have to fight your own battles. Deal with it.' Yes, I would, thanks a lot. But how? What was going on? What was wrong with Emma? I was her friend, I wanted to be her friend more than anything. She knew

142

that, didn't she? Tears, sleeplessness, unsettled fits of light and nightmarish sleep.

In my class in primary school, there had been a girl called Ciara, with freckles and short red hair in a bob, held back at the sides with little blue slides with white polka dots on them. Her mam used to collect her after school every day because she thought the twenty-minute walk home to her estate was too far and dangerous. Her mam worked part time, and the year I was nine, she used to be late every Thursday, so Ciara had to wait at the school door for twenty minutes after all the other kids had gone home. She had two little sisters, twins, but they finished early and went to someone's house or something like that. I used to see her there as I made my solitary way home, through the gate set in the high grey wall, across the road and around the corner.

After a month or so, Ciara called me over and asked me to play with her while she waited. I was thrilled, and managed to play hopscotch without fucking up. So after that, I would play with Ciara every Thursday after school. During the days, she would play with her best friend, Niamh, and the other girls and wouldn't even come over to me and say hello.

One lunchtime I went up to her when she was playing marbles in the yard, my own marbles heavy in my coat pocket. I was testing the idea in my head, that while there were girls that weren't nice, there were other girls who never said anything to me at all, and maybe some of them were girls who were nice, but were so happy and busy playing with their own friends that they didn't notice I had nobody, only if I took the first step and approached them, things might be different. I had seen it happen last week on an American sitcom that all the kids watched, where this cute little boy in playschool who had no friends walked up with his train to another boy with a train and said, 'That's a nice train, I have one too. Why don't we play a game with them?' 'Sure, I'd love to,' and they romped away, the words coming up over them and their smiling teacher. That had stayed in my mind ever since. Maybe it could work for me. But as I stood nervously beside Ciara, she turned from where she was lining up her shot, irritated and impatient at the interruption.

'What?'

She wasn't pleased to see me. Stupid Cassandra, haven't you learned that things can't really be fixed like that. Trying just makes you feel worse.

'Nothing,' I said and walked away.

I was afraid she wouldn't even play with me on Thursday, but she called me over and played marbles with me, and I was so relieved, I didn't mind losing all my nice marbles to her. Even the big rainbow one that had cost a week's pocket money and was my favourite; it was gorgeous. I used to think it looked like the oil that leaks from cars after it's been raining and the colours on the ground are all translucent and streaked like a rainbow only nicer, pinkier and more purply, all mixed up together, like waves in a crystal ball. I used to stare at it for hours, turning it around and around in the palm of my hand. But I was a very bad player, no matter how hard I practised at home.

Next day I heard someone admiring Ciara's new marbles in the classroom.

'Where did you get them?'

'I won them off Cassandra.'

'Oh, well then.'

As in, oh well then, that wasn't much bother to you, was it, winning them off that dopey eejit. But at least I had her Thursdays, and if that went well, who knew what might happen.

And so it went on. When Ciara's birthday came up she handed out her invitations to most of the girls in the class, except the ones she was fighting with. I didn't expect one, so I stared at the desk – seeing invitations always upset me. No one ever invited me. But Ciara came over to me. 'My mam said to invite you,' and walked away.

It was the best surprise I'd ever had, even if it only came from her mam, who always said hello, it's very nice of you, to wait with Ciara like this. My parents were pleased, saying how great it was that I had found a friend. I explained that she only played with me on Thursday, but they said that was a good beginning.

I wanted to go, I wanted it to be good, and on the Saturday afternoon, I dressed in my best clothes – blue velvet dress with pink frills, pink tights, blue shoes, and a blue ribbon with pink dots for my hair. I thought I looked great, but I regretted it the minute I walked into the sitting room with my present, and saw that the others were just wearing better versions of their normal clothes with maybe clean hair and a ribbon, and I looked so out of place. They all just looked at me, as if to say, fucking eejit, what's she doing here, look at the state of her, and only Ciara's mam said what a beautiful dress. But Ciara liked the present, a blue hairband with silky material flowers all up it and a board game featuring her favourite cartoon characters. She

145

put the hairband on and everyone admired her, so I was pleased. And we all played games organised by her mam like pass-the-parcel and musical chairs, so they had to play with me and I felt better.

The party was nice, pink plastic 'Happy Birthday' tablecloth, matching paper plates and white plastic cups filled with Coke and lemonade, chocolate and sweets, Rice Krispie buns, all laid out on the plates, presided over by Ciara, her mam running around, mopping up spillages and so on. Then she went out of the room to deal with Ciara's sisters, who were acting up because they couldn't eat with us. They'd been fed their share already and the room was too small to squeeze them in. We were crowded enough as it was.

I panicked once her mam was gone, but nothing happened, people just chatted away. Then one girl said, 'This is a great party, Ciara.' There was a cluster of agreements, what a nice party, what a nice girl she was for inviting them all, and then, what a nice girl for inviting Cassandra, that nobody liked. I looked at her, desperately hoping for I don't know what.

'Yes,' she said smugly. 'Amn't I nice for inviting someone I don't like.'

I swallowed the Rice Krispie bun in my mouth without chewing. It caught and burned and tore at my throat and I coughed and coughed my throat dry, eyes dry and stinging, her mam rushing back in, worried, giving me a drink when I calmed down, the others having left to watch the video.

'I feel sick,' I said, imploring her for help with my eyes, not knowing what to say to her.

'Do you want to go home?'

'Yeah.'

So she rang home, and my dad collected me and drove me home, and brought me into the kitchen where my mam was, and seeing the scissors and Sellotape and the bits of left-over wrapping paper sitting on the dresser where I'd put them only this morning made me burst out, saying it's not fair, I hate the place and they hate me. I don't want to go back there ever again. Why can't you do something?

'We'll go in to the teachers and talk to them again.'

'That's worse, you went in before the summer holidays last year, and the ones beside me kept talking to me in the middle of class and I talked back because no-one ever talked to me, and teacher got cross the day after you went in and gave me lines and told me to get you to sign them and to see what you thought of that.'

'Well she was an old bag and she's left, and you've a nicer teacher now.'

'It still doesn't matter, I'd a nice teacher before and she couldn't make them play with me, and why should someone have to make them play with me? What's wrong with me?'

'Nothing, pet, it's them that has problems, not you.'

'Well how come they've friends and I don't?'

'You have friends here on this road.'

'Why can't I go to school with them?'

But it was no good, and I knew it. The schools here were full, and I wouldn't get in, and things would go on like they always did. Talking just made my parents upset, and there was nothing they could do anyway. It was my

147

own fault, only I didn't know how to make myself a decent person. I still didn't.

CHAPTER 16

School again, same as yesterday, only instead of disappearing at little break, I decided to follow Emma and talk to her. She and Linda and Natasha went into the hall. They pulled grey plastic-backed chairs over to the radiators and sprawled all over them. I walked over to them, and they got up and walked away. I was so nervous I tripped over someone's bag, and when I looked up they'd gone. I couldn't find them.

Lunchtime, I followed them into the hall. They got up and left the room. Too embarrassed to follow them out, I sat down where they'd got up and ate two bites from my sandwich. Then I put it away and left.

I saw them going into the nice toilets and I followed them. They picked their bags off the pastel pink tiles and walked out again. This was the most blatant snub of all. They were so close to me, forced by the confined space almost, but taking care not to, to touch against me as they brushed past. And it was too painful to call out to Emma. My friend.

I locked myself in a toilet. I couldn't think. I stared at the large roll of pink toilet paper attached to the wall, trailing on the ground, walked into the floor, dirty and messy and torn and wet. The cleaners couldn't have got this far yet. The pink-tinted see-through plastic roll container was set in the solid concrete wall. The wall looked like pale white-and-pink marbley stone and divided this cubicle from the next. Only the walls didn't reach right up to the ceiling. Not enough privacy for me. I closed my eyes. I stayed there until the toilets filled up with the back-to-class rush and someone knocked on the door because I'd been there so long none of them had seen me go in, and I said 'out in a minute', flushed the toilet, made some noises to indicate I'm-fixing-my-clothes-now and walked out.

Back to class. Sit at my desk and flinch as Emma walks past. Glued to my history book. Back home. Sit in my room preparing and strengthening myself to talk to Emma in the morning. It'll be Wednesday, the half-day, that won't be so bad, no long embarrassing lunch break. In again. Emma's in. Flinch without looking up as she passes by my desk.

Follow them without their seeing me at little break. They sit in a cloakroom. An enclosed area, they'll have to walk past me to get away. But this time you have to ask her, this time you have to do it, no matter what.

I approached the cloakroom soundlessly, creeping along by the white-washed wall. I could hear what they were saying now.

'Thanks for sticking by me like this,' Emma was saying in a sweetly dignified and grateful voice, like an impoverished aristocrat taken in and fed by her former kitchen hands.

'It's the least we can do,' Natasha said soothingly. 'Have you made any big decisions yet?'

'No, but at least I've managed to stop myself slashing Cassandra's wrists with the kitchen knife.'

'Well, you can't blame yourself for thinking like that after what she did to you.'

'I know.'

'You just have to pull yourself together, and the sooner you stop smoking so much blow all the time you'll be in better form for making plans.'

'I need it for my nerves though, I'm in fucking bits, I am, and she did this to me.'

Enough, Cassandra, you've heard enough. Pick up your bag, and get out. Get out of this place now. Thank God it's raining. Nobody in the street will notice your streaming tears as you sneak out and hurry down the road, as long as you don't make a sound. Go. No one can see you. Run home, just as well you're in the door, you can't control the crying anymore.

'What's wrong, love, what happened?'

'I can't go back there, Mum, I just can't do it, they all hate me, and it's serious this time, they all hate me because of Emma, they're all saying I did something to her, something bad.'

'And what does she say?'

'She won't come near me, and I heard her saying a minute ago that she wanted to slash my wrists with the kitchen knife.'

I cried then, told all that had happened this week, and didn't say a word for the rest of the day; fell asleep where I was in the kitchen. I woke up in the middle of the night and found I was in my bed, I went to the toilet, then went back to bed and slept for the rest of the night.

CHAPTER 17

When I woke up, it was eleven o'clock in the morning. I wanted to stay where I was, but I was starving, and hunger got the better of me.

When I went downstairs, my mother was sitting in the kitchen. Drinking coffee at the oak table. The lights were on because the day was dark outside, a grey sky with wind and rain lashing against the windows.

'How are you feeling?'

'Okay, but I'm not going to school.'

'It's alright, your dad went in and saw them. He said you wouldn't be in today.'

'He'd better not have told them, Mum.'

'He said you were very upset – told them what you told us.'

'I didn't want them to know.'

'This has to be sorted out. Things have gone far enough.'

'What did they say?'

'Oh, they were shocked. They'd had no idea what was going on. They called in some of the girls and discussed it with them.'

'What did they do that for?'

'To get a better idea of the situation.'

'And did they?'

'Well, maybe they did. But the only advice they could give us was to do nothing, and it would all blow over.'

Of course. Teachers were stupid. Couldn't handle anything. I said nothing. Just stared at the rain on the window. My mother sat there, trying to act competent. Thinking what to say and how to say it.

'So your dad told them that just wasn't good enough. Said we hadn't paid out good money for you to go there so that something like this could happen right under their noses.'

I looked her in the face this time, still not saying anything. So it came down to money, did it? If you paid, these things didn't happen. You went to school with decent people. You got taken care of properly.

'Don't worry, pet. We'll take care of everything. You don't have to go back there ever again. We'll find a good school for you. You just stay here and take it easy for a few days.'

'That's not the point and you know it.'

She looked confused. 'Of course it is, love. The important thing is to get you away from Emma.'

'No. The important thing is for me to understand why this happened. Why these things always happen to me.'

And she couldn't tell me that. None of them could. Fucking adults. They knew nothing, but thought they had the right to make you do whatever they wanted. I went straight back to my room.

The more I thought about it, the angrier I became. When I was a kid, I used to think a nice school would fix everything. Now it seemed to me that people were just as bad everywhere. It didn't matter where I went because I knew that I'd feel the same anywhere. The ways things were, I'd never trust anyone again, and my parents were too stupid to see that. I'd just have to sort this out myself. And now. I'd been depressed too long.

So think. Start at the beginning, when Emma was your friend. And yet she couldn't have been, ever. Not to treat me like this. I remembered how I'd always done things her way. I used to think it was normal give and take of a friendship, but it had felt wrong, and I had covered this up to myself, thinking that I didn't know what normal behaviour was, anyway. Remember how Mick and Brian said she was a two-faced bitch and why? Remember how she manipulated her mother? Admit it. She used and manipulated you too and you should have known that all along. But I was so desperate to be friends with her, to be like her. I wanted her so much I ignored all the signs. I should have seen this coming.

Emma was friends with me because she needed someone in school to hang around with and load all her insecurities onto. Having complete control over me no matter how far she pushed me, increased her self-esteem and gave her an outlet for all her emotions.

Because Emma's very insecure, I know that. Her mother keeps hassling her about school. She hates the fact that the other girls do better than her. She hates them for being rich and justifies her hatred by calling them snobs. Why shouldn't she hate me all the more because I only ever wanted to be her friend?

But what had made her do this to me now? Why hadn't she just let things go on as before? The only bad thing that had happened to her recently that I knew of was the break-up with Paul, and that had nothing to do with me. I remembered how I'd nearly lost her over him. But it wasn't my fault he thought I was better-looking than her. And she'd got him in the end. Even still, Natasha had hated me ever since Gary had asked me up. At the time, Emma had told me that Natasha was jealous. More than likely, Emma was jealous too. She hated me because she was jealous of everything I was that she wanted to be. And if that was true now, then it had probably been the same when I was a kid.

I dried my eyes. Then I cried some more. I was one stupid bitch. Emma had never been my friend, nor Brenda, they were too alike. They had never liked me, and I was thick enough to think they could. Too stupid for anyone to like me, ever. Would have been a lot better if I'd never been born. Should have been aborted or strangled at birth.

It's up to you now. What do you want to do? Kill yourself and get it over with? No, they'd all just laugh at me even more, saying fucking eejit, she doesn't even have the guts to face up to her own problems. And Emma could act the martyr even more. 'She couldn't live with the guilt after what she did to me,' she'd say. 'Don't worry,' the class and Kilmore would soothe her, 'What can you expect from someone who didn't have the guts to face up to her own actions?'

I still didn't even know what I was supposed to have done to Emma. So what if the adults knew the rumours weren't true. They teach you from the day you're born that you have to be independent: you make friends, go to school, work hard, get into college, study hard, make more friends, get a job, get married – or not get married, suit yourself. All this about education and friends and if you fuck up, one or the other or both you're not supposed to think it's your own fault?

Your friends are meant to be there for you for the rest of your life. But they don't like you because you're more intelligent and better off. Or else they're the same as you, but they don't like you because you didn't give them a chance to get to know you. And you're supposed to be able to sort this out?

Okay, maybe I didn't give the other girls a chance. But I can think what I want to, and I still think they study too hard, even if it's not their fault, they feel they have to. In Kilmore they're better fun, only the problem is they're insecure because their parents have the same values as the parents here, only less money so there's more pressure. People like Emma doubt themselves, so they have a good time and try to forget about it. Families who are bigger snobs than around here because they want their kids to be better than everyone else. No matter how nice her mam was to you, you knew those were her values. You've been idealising these places too long.

People like Emma wanted to please their parents but doubted they could and were too lazy to put in the effort anyway. So they said they didn't want to be like that. They wanted their freedom – good time, cigarettes, drink, blow. That was easy. Grief in school – school's boring, no use to you at all. Shit from your parents and you answer back with direct quotes from your favourite songs – you've got to accept me for what I am. I am what I am and I refuse to conform to the system like you do.

Only people like me heightened their insecurities. So they hated us. Withheld their friendship and tormented us. People like me in my school, put away in a little box – don't bother, not worth knowing. But how was Emma supposed to deal with me? I thought wanting her so badly would make things alright, but it didn't. It made things worse, because I was everything her mother and her friends wanted rolled into one. The ideal, if there's such a thing in this world. But there isn't, and I had one big weak spot which explained why she was friends with me and why she hated me at the same time. I wanted her to like me. I would do anything so that she would like me. And she exploited that, pushing me to see how far I'd go, despising me more every time. Knowing I wanted her more than anything.

Emma used me. Fucking me around made her feel better about herself. All the little things: borrowing money that was never given back, wanting me to wear clothes I didn't like, jewellery that gave me a rash, make-up that didn't suit, turning up late. All the big things: Kev, Paul, last week, this.

It all made perfect sense. I could even see why all the girls in school believed the rumours. None of them knew me at all because I never talked to them. Admit it, you were asking for it.

But you have to get over it. You can't go through life like this.

I've come to one decision by Sunday night. I can't do

anything else until I know what Emma has said about me. I know she's not my friend, but the thought of her hurts more than anything. I'm not even sure I could turn her away if she wanted me to take her back, so I have to fix the mess in school. I don't know how I'm going to do that, but I'll have a better idea when I know what's going on.

The only one I feel I can turn to is Michelle. The one image I've kept in my head to convince myself there are good people out there is that of Michelle, telling Emma not to say one more bad word about me or she'd bust her and then never talk to Emma again. Of course I was taking a risk with her. Emma could have made her hate me too. But maybe not. And if not, she'd help me. She might or might not know what was going on, but she could find out.

CHAPTER 18

I knew what I was going to do when I got up on Monday. It was up to me to sort this one out, and while the idea terrified me, the prospect of just letting things hang was infinitely worse. Problem was, I didn't know Michelle's second name. I knew her address, 44 Rosebrook, but that was no good to me, because without a second name I couldn't ring her up and ask her. I was so desperate I rang up Directory Enquiries and begged them to give me the number with just the address, but of course they wouldn't, or shouldn't, or couldn't do that. It meant I'd have to get on a bus to Kilmore and knock on her door, hoping to God I'd catch her in one of the rare moments these people were to be found in their homes.

The thought of it scared me shitless. I might run into Emma or Brenda, even though it was a different part of Kilmore. So what, though – they were, after all, ignoring me, and they were hardly going to cross the road to ask me what I was doing there. Fuck them. Go today? No, it's raining, and if she's not there, you have to walk around or something until she's supposed to be back. You have to see her. Alright then, but tomorrow, it has to be tomorrow, you can't wait any longer.

The doorbell rang at about five o'clock. Only strangers

went to the upstairs door, but even so, I was completely stunned to see Sinéad and Tessa standing there. I stood in silence, not knowing whether their being here was a good or a bad thing.

'We were worried about you when you didn't come into school,' Sinéad said, as if they'd worked this one out before walking in the gate.

'Did you expect me to?'

That was good, it left things to go one way or the other. Were they on Emma's side or mine?

Sinéad answered in a nervous flood almost at once. 'No, you must have guessed what was going on, what they were all saying. We didn't know what to say to you, and by the time we'd worked out that we'd tell you what was happening after break on Wednesday, you were gone, and we felt really bad.'

They looked sincere, they probably were. Remember, the rumours spread to the general public on Tuesday, and from then till Wednesday wasn't long for figuring out what you're going to say to someone in an embarrassing situation. No matter how long it had seemed to me. You should hate yourself for laughing at them and belittling them behind their backs. Like Emma. You don't deserve to have them standing there in the cold, the wind blowing into the hall that was warm until I opened the door.

'It's freezing out here. Come in and have a cup of tea or coffee or something.'

I led them down to the kitchen, thankful there was no-one else in the house. I tried to fill the awkward silence by boiling the kettle and getting cups out and so on, getting my head together.

'So,' I said, as we all sat around the table looking at each other, our coffee too hot to knock back in procrastinating gulps. 'So, what exactly is being said about me?'

'Nobody really knows,' Tessa said tentatively.

'Nobody knows? I go through hell over something nobody knows?'

'Well, what I mean is, nobody knows what you've done, except Emma, Linda and Natasha. Linda and Natasha just told everyone you'd done something terrible to Emma, and looking at the state she's in, everybody believed them, because they didn't know you. Except us, and a few others.'

Everybody knows it's bad, but they don't know what it is. Oh, Jesus, what in the name of God is it? I was never so pissed off in my life. And sick of it. Sick of the pettiness, the pointing finger, the ostracism, what they call 'the small-town mentality' in books and films and songs, when the big heroes talk about feeling oppressed by the closed minds all around them, having to escape to the big city. Only the city was just as bad. Worse, because at least in the country you could go off on your own to the middle of nowhere and sit in a field or something to avoid people. Here, they were everywhere. No getting away from them. I was sick, sick to death of all this.

'So, I've done nothing, no one knows what I've done, and everyone hates me for it.'

'They don't hate you, it's just . . .'

'No-one knows me, so they don't know what to think.'

Quick Cassandra, you're beginning to bore yourself with all this repetition. Get this sorted out now. But I was half-way there, I wasn't completely alone now. I smiled.

'Well, I've been thinking over what to do and . . .'

162

CHAPTER 19

The rain had gone by the following morning, though the weather was cooler and still windy. The sun was shining, in a clear blue sky that had lost all the warmth of the summer. Seeing as it was such a crisp dry day, I didn't have any excuses to put off my trip even if I wanted to.

A bus drew up the minute I got to the stop, and I got on, wondering if the gods had intervened to make the day run so smoothly. Things continued to go my way. I ran into no one I knew in Kilmore. I found my way to Michelle's estate easily enough. Very bleak and grey, sprawling monotonous roads of identical little houses. You'd be lost if you didn't follow the numbers on the houses and match up the names of the roads to the directions learned off by heart in your head because everywhere looks exactly the same. You wouldn't know where you were. I stood nervously on the doorstep of Michelle's house, praying that things wouldn't turn sour on me now. They didn't. Michelle came to the door, with Jane behind her.

'Cassandra,' said Michelle, surprise followed by relief and concern. 'I've been wanting to get in touch with you these last few weeks, but there was no way of contacting you, come on in.'

I followed her in through a madhouse of brothers and brothers' friends and parents and neighbours, so crowded I didn't get a look at the place, and into her bedroom, tiny, but the only empty room in the house. Painted white with posters all over the walls. We sat on her bed.

'How've you been?' they asked. They obviously had some of idea of what was going on.

I ran through how Emma'd been a bitch to me pretty much the whole week she'd been going with Paul, but I'd put up with it, thinking she was just going through a bad patch, and she'd been on the hop most of that week anyway, so I hadn't seen her. Then, Tuesday two weeks ago, I'd got a call from Emma to say she'd broke up with Paul, he'd been doing the dirty on her. I didn't speak to her the rest of the week because her mam said she was too sick to come to the phone, and when she came back to school, she'd ignored me, as well as the whole class, and then I found out it was because I'd done something on her. And that was why I'd come over here, to find out what.

'We never thought she'd go that far, we just thought she was giving you grief,' Michelle said. 'And we weren't even sure of that. You're going to laugh when you hear all it was. Just Emma being stupid and trying to put the blame on other people. You.'

'I don't know if you know this, but Emma was shagging Paul from the first night she went off with him,' Jane said, with an air of, I know this sounds bad, and unbelievable, but believe me it's true. 'My fella Mick overheard them talking about it, saying it was right for them, it felt right, they were in love, then Emma told me herself later . . .'

'What? She didn't even tell me.'

'No, it wasn't like that. Just listen. Emma was shagging Paul that week, and I knew and Mick knew he had another girlfriend. We told her, but she wouldn't believe us because I was hanging around with Michelle now, and her and Michelle were fighting.'

'She told me that, said it was over me.'

'Yeah, her and Paul came into Johnny's pissed one night, and broke it to Kev loudly that you weren't going with him, so of course he was fucking scarlet because everyone was listening and he'd told them all you were going with him. So he said, so what, you were frigid anyway, and they laughed, and Emma started mouthing off about you, real bitchy, and real loud how you'd never had a fella, and so on, and Paul was laughing, saying just as well he didn't have a frigid girlfriend, and things were getting real bad, so I pulled her out and shut her mouth for you.'

'That's not how she said it.'

'I bet she didn't. She's a real sly two-faced bitch, probably said she was standing up for you or something. I used to like her, then I got to see what she was like. But she was never ever this bad before, otherwise I'd have warned you not to go near her.'

'Mick and Brian warned me. I should have listened to them.'

'Don't worry about it. No one else said anything. How were you to know what to think.'

Silence fell. Jane picked up the thread of the story. 'Then Emma found out the following Tuesday that he really did have another girlfriend and she was in bits. I saw her that weekend and she looked awful. Then me and

Michelle saw her again on the Monday night, and she looked worse. But this was just passing each other in the street sort of thing. And we said nothing to her. Then on Tuesday night we were sitting on a wall in the village, just dossing and having a smoke, and she came up to us, totally out of it, like she'd just been drinking and smoking blow, you could smell it off her. And she said, "Please talk to me, don't hate me, talk to me, please," and she started crying, real desperate. Her hair and clothes were a state, and she'd gone all spotty. And she was in such a state that we took pity on her, me and Michelle, and said "it's alright Emma, we don't hate you, what's wrong with you?" And we sat her down and comforted her and stuff, and she said "I think I'm pregnant." '

I was horrified, and stayed silent, searching in their unreadable faces for some clue of the outcome to all of this and where I fitted in. No wonder Emma had looked so awful, but while I felt horror for what she must have gone through, I was just as horrified at myself for feeling, good, it serves her right.

Jane continued. 'We were more surprised to hear this than we should have been, because she'd only been shagging him for just over a week, and this was only a week or so after they'd broken up. So we said are you sure, and she said yes, I always get my flowers on the same day every month, and I was supposed to get them on Thursday but I didn't. Well, you never know, we said, it's still early days yet, did you use a condom? And she said yes, but it burst one night and she cried some more. And we felt so sorry for her.'

I was feeling sympathy for her too. Michelle gave me a

166

look as if to say don't feel sorry for her now, wait until you hear what comes next.

Jane paused for dramatic effect. 'Then I said to her, why did she do it, because most of us wouldn't, even with someone we'd been going out with for months, and even a total slut our age would never ever do it on the first night. Whatever about older people and people in films and stuff. We were shocked when we heard about Emma in the first place, really really shocked. And she said, "I had to do it to keep him." '

' "No you didn't," I told her. "Only a total bastard'd make you do something like that." '

' "Yes I did." Emma went on. "The big problem is that an eighteen-year-old has different expectations to a fourteen-year-old, and he wouldn't have had anything to do with me if I hadn't told him from the first conversation that Saturday night when he wanted Cassandra and I said she wasn't here, that he didn't want her anyway, she was frigid, she'd only met one fella in her life, and that was scumbag Kev, and he laughed and said he was better off with me so, and I said yes. She's a stupid bitch, all the fellas stop and stare at her in the street, but she's as dozey and dry-arse as they come, she didn't even get her flowers until about three months ago, she'd never had a drink in her life until she came here." '

I was crying and I didn't care. I hated her, or thought I did, and I hated myself too, for not having seen through her. I longed for what I thought had been and had hoped would be, and painfully wrenched that ideal out of me, but wondered as I spat it out if all that was good and worth hanging around for in life was going out with it, leaving nothing behind but bitterness. And I was too young for that, wasn't I?

Michelle picked up the story where Jane had left off. 'I wish I could tell you it doesn't get any worse, but it does. I said, "Leave Cassandra out of this, what has she got to do with it?"

' "She has fucking everything to do with it, I blame her for this. If I'm pregnant, then it's her fault."

' "Really," I said. "I must be a bit slow or something, why is it her fault?"

' "It's obvious, isn't it? If it hadn't have been for her, I wouldn't have had to shag Paul, not so soon anyway, I would have had time to get the Pill, but as it was, it was me or her, and he'd only have me if I wasn't frigid like her." '

That was it. That was the Big Thing. The Horrific Crime. It was pathetic. It was the most pathetic thing I'd ever heard.

'Pathetic, isn't it,' Jane said. 'That's what we told her, and she said, "No, you're just saying that because you like her better than me. It's her fault. I wish I'd never been stupid enough to bring her out here, then he'd never have seen her and I wouldn't have this problem." We just got up and walked off. We couldn't take anymore.'

'If it hadn't have been for me she'd never have met him in the first place.'

'Try telling her that, she'd either say, "good, I wouldn't have shagged him then," or "so what, I would have met him eventually." She's hopeless.'

'Is she pregnant?'

'No, she came around here last night wanting to sort

168

things out, saying she got her flowers and everything's alright again. We told her to fuck herself.'

'Yeah, that's a hundred per cent,' Michelle said and we had a good laugh over that one.

What a stupid bitch that Emma was. Seeing the situation for what it was made me feel a lot better. This was truly pathetic. All my life I'd thought these people were cleverer than me, and because of that I'd feared them for what they could do to me, idolised them, copied them, tried to find motives for their actions, looked down on myself the way they looked down on me, tormented myself like they tormented me. I could never ever be good enough, even to lick the dogshit off the soles of their shoes. When really they were stupid. Emma was stupid, insecure and jealous. She was so stupid that she thought up something as pathetic as this and punished me for it. And I was so angry with myself for not realising it before, for tying myself up in knots over people with sweet fuck-all between their ears. A lifetime of delusions.

'So all this grief in school, Emma hating me, everyone ignoring and hating me was all over nothing.'

'That's about the size of it,' said Michelle. 'But what I don't understand is how she got away with it.'

'I do, I bet I do. You see, in our school they're sort of swotty and don't do much, and the idea of drinking and blow and sex and stuff, even though they wouldn't do any of it and'd sort of disapprove of and look down on and laugh at people like that, well, it still has a sort of attraction for them. Like, they might say it's not mad, but they don't know that. And there's always the chance that it really is mad and if it is, then there's the chance that there's all these mad people out there having the time of their lives, and real life is just passing them by and them slogging away at school, growing up inexperienced and knowing nothing. Youse can laugh, because to youse a night knacker-drinking is just the best crack going, and that's it. It might even piss you off a bit when it's cold or raining and there's someone puking their guts up beside you, or if it's you puking your guts up, whatever. And to them, if it were adults it wouldn't be mad, but it's different when you're talking about people your own age. Especially when you've never done it, and all you have are snatches of gossip and rumour blown up and totally unrecognisable by the time they reach you, only you don't know that, how could you know that? I'd say that Emma must have told Linda and Natasha what she told you, pregnant, and all Cassandra's fault, because they didn't like each other before, but Natasha's hated me since, it's a long story, but she really hates me.'

My God, I don't care that she hates me. It used to hurt me, even though I didn't like her, because I wanted people to like me and anyone's dislike hurt. Now I don't give a shit if the whole world hates me, because if they're all like that then they're not worth it. But they're not all like that, here's Michelle and Jane, genuinely nice, and of course, Sinéad and Tessa. I smiled again.

'So, the fact that she hates me, and, why not, the added satisfaction of seeing Emma, the mad thing they hadn't been good enough for hitting rock bottom, would have made them take Emma under their wing. Protecting her from me. Seeing Emma looking awful, stoned on blow, validated by Linda and Natasha, would have led the others to believe I'd done something, seeing as they didn't really know me very well.'

They considered it, and I thought it over again, proudly convinced that that was indeed what had happened.

'That's deadly, I'd say you're right,' they agreed.

As did Sinéad and Tessa, when they called over that night as arranged.

'So what are you going to do about it?' They wanted to know.

I thought the best idea would be just to let the truth spread itself around naturally and let that take care of itself. Start it rolling with Sinéad and Tessa, a few phonecalls, then sit back and wait for the multiple chain effect.

I even got some apologetic phonecalls back that evening from friends of Sinéad and Tessa, which I accepted graciously. I was ashamed of how I'd written them all off in the past. I was relieved how easy this was, and disgusted at how easily balances could be redressed the opposite way, how easily public opinion could be swayed, for you and against you. Talk about potentially lethal implications. Calm down, these are extenuating circumstances, you know that. Sadness and desolation. It would take a while to get over this one, and it wasn't over yet. Not everyone knew, that would be dealt with in school tomorrow, when Linda and Natasha were told. Then human nature would take its course.

CHAPTER 20

I was still terrified of going back to school. Terrified that some people wouldn't believe me, say it was Emma's word against mine. Yes, I could prove it. Yes, loads were already on my side. Yes, Sinéad and Tessa would back me up. Yes, they had a lot more credibility than Linda and Natasha. But who knew, who ever knows?

Sinéad and Tessa told me, when they met me at the school gates like we'd arranged, that Linda and Natasha had just been set straight about things by their friend Nuala outside the first class. But no, they hadn't denied anything. I had thought as much in my positive version of how things could turn out.

The facts were consistent with Emma's version. They'd known from the beginning how flimsy and stupid the whole story sounded, that was why they'd shrouded it in secrecy. The only chance they had now was to pretend to be outraged and say they'd been just as deceived as everyone else. And that was what they'd done. How were they supposed to know what had really happened, they said. They'd never been to Kilmore, or met any of these people, they just knew what they were told. And seeing Emma like that, they could well believe it. And they couldn't have checked it out either. How could they, they'd promised not to say a word . . .

'What do people think of them now?' I asked.

'Pretty much the same as they always did. Like, everyone always thought they were sound enough and harmless. So now, well, they're all sort of saying, it was still mean of them, but Emma must have been really convincing, and Natasha didn't like you anyway since Gary fancied you so it would have been that much easier for her to believe it. Which is what Natasha was telling them herself when we came out here,' Sinéad said, looking from me to Tessa for confirmation on this one.

Tessa was walking backwards and forwards shivering, hands deep in the pockets of her gabardine. The place was getting busy, loads of girls walking through the gates. It must be getting close on nine.

'So what about Emma?'

Sinéad looked at Tessa, then took her glasses off and wiped them. Tessa stopped walking and leaned against the railings looking directly at me. 'Emma's a touchy enough situation,' she said. 'People are horrified at how she treated you. But they feel really, really sorry for what she must have gone through with Paul. Even if it was her own fault and she did want to shag him. It's still awful for her to have thought she was pregnant, and they say that's punishment enough for anyone. A lot of them say that probably explains why she did it to you, that she had to feel someone else was to blame other than herself, it would've been too much for her to cope with otherwise.'

'That was it, was it? I suppose that's why she was

173

treating me like shit before that as well,' I said sarcastically. But I wasn't surprised. They didn't look surprised either.

'They don't know the full story. And would you want them to? They'd say you brought it on yourself, putting up with it for so long.'

'I know, they'd think I was a real fucking eejit. And they'd be right. But I just can't believe they're coming out of this all perfect and innocent. It's not fair,' I said bitterly.

They shrugged their shoulders. 'That's life,' Sinéad said. 'It's one thing getting all self-righteous and pointing the finger, but when the tables are turned, like in this, they're all as bad as Linda and Natasha. Okay, not as bad, because they didn't have the facts. But they still shouldn't have behaved like they did, even if it did look bad, and they know that. So they feel guilty and want to forget about it as quickly as possible. But they can't do that until Emma, Linda and Natasha are forgiven, because otherwise they'll be reminded of it every time they see them in school. Better to forget.'

'I see.' I knew Sinéad was right but it still pissed me off.

'It's nothing to get angry about,' Tessa said. 'Just give them a chance.'

You know they're right. You don't? Well, it doesn't matter, because you have to believe them. And it's nine now anyway so you have to go in. Everyone else has. The place is deserted and there's a teacher going on the door to give out little white late forms.

We walked in past her. 'What about Emma, what am I going to do about her – nothing?'

'Nothing. Just stay away from her.'

I walked into the classroom. I read WELCOME BACK,

174

SORRY ABOUT EVERYTHING scrawled in pink chalk across the blackboard. Everybody clapped. They really did mean it and they wanted me to know it. They wanted to be friends.

I'd never seen good qualities in them before, or in anyone else, apart from Michelle, Jane, Sinéad and Tessa. I thought I'd found friendship in Emma and Brenda but I hadn't. I went looking for it when it'd been here all the time. Linda and Natasha even had the decency to apologise.

Then the teacher came in, and smiled, understanding the message before dispelling it in a cloud of dust with the well-worn duster. Yes, teacher, stick that one in the staff-room pipe and smoke it. Now you don't have to worry about 'intervention', and dealing with pissed-off parents when you fuck up. But it's not like primary school, where the teachers should have helped. You even sat right under their fucking noses so that they could see you. So many things should have spoken for themselves. Now you're older and these things are more difficult. Teenagers guard their world closely and fiercely. Live in it and rule it by a set of conventions passed on by older teenagers, whose behaviour they observe and absorb. Insulated from the outside, especially teachers, who fuck up so much of their life as it is with school and homework and study and exams. Not that children don't want their own way when it comes to friends, but they're only little kids, they're too young to know better. And they might have seemed like monsters to me, but to the adults they'd have been only little kids. There'd been no justification for what had ever happened to me. No, the teachers couldn't have done a lot this time around. But things should work themselves out now. Yes, teacher. I was embarrassed at the thought of her saying anything, but she started the class as if nothing had happened.

Ten minutes into the class, Emma walked in, looking physically in as good a shape as she'd ever been. I thought I'd just feel anger and hatred when I saw her, but a wave of burning sadness walloped and stung me. I wanted to run up to her and beg her to be my friend again, no matter what. And the terrible nerves, the feelings of inadequacy, that I wasn't good enough for her, not now not ever, the overwhelming desire to please her no matter what, like before. And fear, fear of the influence she still had on me, of the damage she was still capable of causing. But I controlled this, calming and soothing myself, it's alright, she's only a bitch, remember how her mind works, as thick as a rock. I couldn't banish the emotions completely, but I managed to stem the flow, to weaken their intensity. And I was alright. Just nervous and uncomfortable.

At the end of the class, I saw her out of the corner of my eye, turn towards Linda and Natasha, who pretended they didn't hear her and walked out of the room. She followed them but couldn't catch them. It was exactly what had happened to me. I hoped she was upset, but I couldn't see her face so I didn't know.

I stuck to Sinéad and Tessa like glue for the rest of the day and stayed well away from Emma, which wasn't difficult, she never came within a hundred yards of me. She adopted a pose like she was real cool and nothing in this place was good enough for her and she stayed like that for the rest of the day. From what I could make out, she wasn't exactly being ignored, but people were much too embarrassed and confused and she looked less approachable than ever. Some did make brief tongue-tied small talk with her, those who were standing beside her as we waited to get into the next class and stuff, but she didn't respond.

After lunch, it was relayed to me that Linda and Natasha'd explained to her upon request why she'd gone out of fashion. She wasn't exactly pleased to have had her personal business splashed around the class. Good, I thought, that's something anyway. When she came to class, she looked more mutinous and aggressive than before. Avoiding social contact with desperate embarrassment. Just the presence of each and every other girl, the eyes cast in her direction, they were like malevolent daggers hurled from all directions. She felt just like I'd felt.

Emma was stoned in school the following morning, and on the hop the next two days. This time she didn't even bother to cover it up, it was like she wanted to get caught. She probably did, so that she'd be expelled; her mam killing her'd be better than personally inflicted social leprosy. Justice. Emma couldn't stand for everyone to know everything in graphic detail. The business made her look like a fool and she knew it. She just didn't want anyone else to know it and the fact that everyone did was too much for her. It gave others more than enough excuse to laugh at her behind her back and she obviously thought that was what was going on. It was all in her head though; not that it mattered to me. I loved seeing her in hell. People were much too embarrassed to talk about her in school, even though at home they probably thought what had happened to her a sordid nightmare of victimisation and devoured it in discussion. Her, mind. The stuff of true life drama, sensationalised fiction, a teenage girl's worst nightmare, naïve young girl exploited. The oldest story in the book, one of the most popular and most derided. Never mind me, no salient details there, nothing to grasp the popular imagination, just conscience-pricking guilt. So I was considered dealt with, gathered and accepted into the fold with love. Case dismissed.

But anger, bitterness, despair and cynicism don't just evaporate. I took comfort in the fact that Emma was suffering, which made me wonder if I could ever be emotionally independent if I was feeding on her pain for my own mental well-being.

That was Friday, and she'd been smoking blow that morning as well, we could all smell it off her.

At lunchtime, I was standing on my own outside the toilets, waiting for Sinéad and Tessa to come out. Emma walked past, I looked down to avoid her eye, but she came straight up to me.

'Cassandra, howya, listen, I'm sorry about everything, and I know you've heard everything and probably hate me now, but I didn't mean it, it's just that I was depressed and pissed off, and worried sick, so I took it all out on you.'

She seemed so sincere, so apologetic, and I knew objectively that she was lying, and I answered the objectively correct answer.

'Fuck off out of my life.'

But I was longing to believe her and make up and I looked into her eyes. I saw it there then, beneath the wounded plea she'd put on for me, all the calculations, assessments, bitchiness. How much she hated me, her jealousy. Everything.

And from then on I was able to separate the real Emma from the other Emma, the one I'd made up in my head that was everything I'd believed of her, everything I'd ever longed for, hoped for. The real Emma, stupid, two-faced, using, who was insecure, jealous and stupid. Thought up stupid excuses to blame me for her problems, remember. And the other Emma, the fantasy Emma, cracked into millions of tiny fragments. And the real Emma was left behind, all her power gone.

Millions of lives are ruined every day because of power. Politicians, dictators, parents, husbands, wives, children, employers, bureaucrats, society and friends. You're not alone, Cassandra. But your life isn't ruined, you wouldn't give that little bitch the satisfaction. Staring her down like this, looking straight into her eyes is exhausting, but she's weakening, she knows you mean it, and she's giving up. The pitiful pleading look is going, she can't keep it up, and she's gone, down the hall.

She's out of my head, she's finally out of my mind and soul. It's gone, she's gone.

On the hop again, and again, no note, not discovered. Homework undone, once, twice, three times. Stoned in the mornings, smoking publicly on school grounds, like she wants to be caught. A test; she sits and stares at the paper, hands up a blank sheet with not even her name written on it, warned by the exiting teacher that severe discipline is imminent.

'Nice one,' she announces, loudly raising her voice

above the general hum of departing girls. 'Maybe they'll expel me if I'm lucky.'

Lunchtime, no summons has arrived and Emma's vocally disappointed.

'The waiting's killing me. Me nerves are at me.'

I assume this means cigarette fumes emanating from the busiest toilets.

Talk about underestimation. Instead, the unmistakable stench of blow, the rumours expanding and thickening like the drifting clouds from within. We're among the first spectators on the scene, arriving to hear Emma shouting aloud to her accompanying teachers as she strides triumphantly along the corridor.

'Deadly, fucking deadly, youse have to expel me now, you've no fucking excuse this time, youse have to kick me out. Hear that everybody? I'm out of this kip, I'm fucking out of here.'

CHAPTER 21

And that was the end of Emma. I never saw her again. On that last day, her mam was called in to take her home. A day later, they called both parents in to discuss Emma's difficulties and recommended that she be 'removed from the school'. I know, because they'd called me in with my own parents earlier in the day to talk about what had been happening so they'd have a better idea of what they were dealing with.

They suggested that Emma be returned to her old school, or, if she'd encounter social difficulties there, be enrolled in a similar school in the area where she'd have a clean break. I heard that from Michelle, when I rang her to tell her what was going on.

She went back to her old class in her old school with Brenda. Michelle and Jane were the only two who knew what had happened and they didn't say anything. In a big school like that, where the class changed with every subject, it was easy to ignore people you didn't like. Not like my cosier, more intimate school. No one heard about the pregnancy or about me. But they all thought she was a mad thing for getting herself expelled, especially the way she did it, she made sure everybody knew about that one. She told those who'd met me and were asking for me that we just didn't get on anymore. She didn't dare go any further, fearing the wrath of Michelle and Jane.

That was the last time I ever heard of Emma. I spoke to Michelle a few times on the phone, but never again after ringing to wish her a happy Christmas. I liked her and Jane a lot but a terrible awkwardness had grown between us. I was embarrassed in front of them for them knowing all that had happened since I met Emma, and they were embarrassed themselves for knowing it and for knowing I was embarrassed for them knowing it.

It might have been the sealing of a great friendship, had we not been so different, had we had something to help us to get over *that*. But all that'd ever be there'd be my old desire to please and be liked by anyone from Kilmore, and the fact that they were good people, so they looked out for me, Michelle in particular, when they saw things going horribly wrong for me.

And so I found myself talking to them, sitting with the phone in my hand, saying nothing, not knowing what to say to them that'd be of interest to them, and vice versa. We just had nothing to say to one another. Of course they were real nice to me and all, taking turns on the phone (Jane was always there when I rang Michelle, the two of them were best friends now). They even asked me to go drinking with them in Kilmore. But I said no. I remembered the good times, but the good times had all been dependent on my thinking I was with friends, and now that was gone, all the good would have gone with it, all the crack of drinking tainted by the situation and location, bitter memories stirring, and I wouldn't be able to relax all night for fear of Emma turning up. So I said no. And eventually we just lost touch.

So I don't know what became of Emma. At first I wished all sorts of terrible fates upon her, but the frustration of not knowing if they'd come to pass, plus the desire to stop thinking about her, to forget, eventually put a stop to my speculation. I reckoned that time, life and her character would take care of revenge for me. She'd have suffered a lot, anway. Her parents would have killed her for getting kicked out of school and that wouldn't have been very nice, coming on top of everything else that had happened to her.

And life went on. Everything settled down to normal and boring again. The Junior Cert was getting closer, and we didn't have time to think about anything else anyway. Even Linda and Natasha were getting worried. It was almost as if Emma had never been, apart from the fact that I now spoke to the class and they to me, and we got on well enough with each other. I even made friends, started walking to school with the ones that walked my way, talking to the ones that sat near me. But the thing is, I didn't care about these things anymore. I'd grown weary of looking for friends just as I was finding them, now that I had them. Two of the best people around, even, Sinéad and Tessa.

There were no hostilities. I was best friend with Sinéad and Tessa like everyone thought I should be — parents, teachers, class. Being friends with them had nothing to do with anyone's expectations. I really liked them, and them me.

It was, after all, what I'd always wanted, friends. Best friends. I should've been happy, shouldn't I? And I was, I was happy, I suppose. Happy that I had Sinéad and Tessa, happy that school was no longer a problem, apart from having to get up in the morning.

But just because on the surface things have been sorted out doesn't mean they go away. You still have to live with yourself and you can't just take a rubber to your head and rub out all that you want to forget.

Sometimes I wake up in terror because I've been dreaming I'm six years old again.

Other times it's Emma.

Occasionally, walking through town on a busy Saturday afternoon, I might catch a glimpse of a girl ahead of me, and something in the dyed hue of her hair, the colour of her clothes, the way she walks, causes me to slow down, swallow down panic and lean back against a shopfront with a beating heart, saying calm down to myself. It's probably not her, and even if it is, so what? And wait for the anger and the threatening tears to die away.

But the older I get, the more I find myself looking at fourteen-year-old girls in a different way. Not at first, because I was still fourteen, and they were the same age, and I was still afraid of girls like Emma when I passed them on the street. But I got older, and they got younger, and I found myself looking at them more and more with sorrow and pity. These girls, with the garish clothes and too much make-up that makes them look younger than they are, even though they think they look great and I used to think they looked great, and they used to laugh at other girls, saying she's gone and done herself up to look older and she

184

looks about twelve instead of fourteen, when they looked just as fresh-faced themselves, in spite of all the bloody make-up. And the older I get, the more I see the signs of insecurity that I never ever saw when I needed to.

The girl waiting for the fella who hasn't turned up yet, posing, trying to look mad, fidgeting with her clothes, desperately smoking with an assumed streetwise attitude, eyes constantly flickering to and from the clock, up and down the road. Another cigarette. And he's coming, a look of overwhelmed relief, before she fixes her face back into blasé nonchalance, and introduces a note of chilled anger around the eyes, but not too much. Just as if to say, you bastard, not that I care whether you turn up or not, I just don't like being fucked around. But she can't keep it up when he gets there. 'You're late,' she says. But that's it, she doesn't push it, otherwise he'll be sick of her bitching and she'll be passed over for another, and she doesn't want that, you can tell, as you watch her walking off into the sunset. Girls like that, who can mess up their lives so easily, with pricks like that, though you shouldn't blame the fellas, it's their own fault. And how many of those girls are there? How many Emmas? How many Cassandras? And I curse myself for having been so fucking stupid.

I think I pity her now and think of her less, even though the memory of those months is as powerful as ever.

Sometimes, on a bad day, sitting silently in a crowded chattering room, panic starts beating in my chest and my head seems to go. I look around at their faces in terror, fearing them, hating them for that, longing to run away and lock myself in an empty room and never have to look at another person again.

Of course I don't, I just sit there, telling myself to stop being so paranoid and neurotic, and it goes.

But otherwise I'm fine. Things really aren't too bad, they could be a lot worse.

I've got more than a lot of people have. A big window to sit at, to watch the rain lash down upon the panes, distorting the view that lies beyond, as I stare at the patch of blue, widening between the banks of grey, wondering at the nature of the sun.